Maddie Hatter and the
DEADLY DIAMOND

penned by
Jayne Barnard

Jayne Barnard (signature)

Maddie Hatter and the
DEADLY DIAMOND

Jayne Barnard

TYCHE BOOKS LTD.

Maddie Hatter and the Deadly Diamond
Published by Tyche Books Ltd.
www.TycheBooks.com

Print ISBN: 978-1-928025-33-7
Ebook ISBN: 978-1-928025-34-4

Cover Art by Robin Robinson
Interior Art by Robin Robinson
Cover Layout by Lucia Starkey
Interior Layout by Ryah Deines
Editorial by M. L. D. Curelas

Author photograph: Kevin Jepson

Alberta
Government

This book was funded in part by a grant from the Alberta Media Fund.

Dedication

To Kevin, who supports my antic imagination in ways beyond counting.

With thanks to the Calgary Steampunks of the Airship's Mess Deck for being such good sports. Special thanks to Monica Willard for the seeds of Maddie's history and a hearty handshake to Andrew Nadon, who inspired Oberon O'Reilly and brought me chocolate.

Contents

The Cornwall Cog and Goggles

POTTY PEER'S AIRSHIP ADRIFT

The expeditionary airship of Baron Bodmin, ardent African explorer, has been found adrift and deserted. Its log-book is missing and no clue remains to its captain's fate.

A fortnight after its last sighting over the mouth of the Suez Canal, the airship appeared off the coast of Cornwall, floating low and rudderless above the waves. No escape canopy or life-vest remained on board. The Coast Guard believes the explorer bailed out over the water and expects the body to come ashore any day now. No trace was found of the fabled Nubian treasure Baron Bodmin sought during his winter's expedition to Egypt.

Chapter One

"I AM VINDICATED." The Honourable Madeleine Main-Bearing danced into her bedchamber with unladylike glee, waving a yellow telegraph flimsy at the room's sole occupant. The clockwork sparrow, half the length of her gloved hand, focused one shiny eye on her as she unpinned her hat and flung it toward her bedpost. "The batty baron's airship has been found adrift near England, abandoned. Suddenly, after months of making me ignore that fascinating fellow's adventure for hats and cravats, CJ wants all my notes about the baron's time in Cairo. Hah!" Maddie fluttered the telegraph again, a thin yellow victory flag, as she pranced across the room. "Let us give him what he asked for, by the ream. Oh, Tweetle-D, there might be a byline for me at last!"

Maddie's name in a London newspaper. The culmination of a dream. Not her real name, naturally, for daughters of Steamlords did not embarrass their families by appearing anywhere but the Society pages, and then only as belles of exemplary style. Her mother had never lived down that Main-Bearing debutante portrait in the Times, under the huge headline: **Peer's Daughter Feared Kidnapped!**

The fashion columns were only permitted by the family because nobody knew who wrote them. But a story like the baron's could not appear under her hats-and-sleeves name. "Miss Maddie Hatter" lacked the dignity to sit atop any paragraph of more import than whether ecru net gloves were permissible for daytime in the heat and dust of Egypt. Maddie needed a new nom-de-plume, a name with gravitas, suitable for the big stories that were sure to be in her future.

First, though, she needed a fast report so CJ could get something into the evening edition. She stripped off her gloves—not ecru netting but plain white, smudged with the orange dust of Cairo streets. Then she retrieved her notebook from a pocket and flipped back the shell-pink cover, ignoring the sequins that spelled, in flowing italic, *"Miss Maddie Hatter, Foreign Fashionista for the London Fog & Cog."*

The Fog was one of several weeklies owned by CJ Kettle's conglomerate, one for every day of the week in some part of England. Although issued a suitably covered notebook for each paper, she found it simpler to carry a single notebook for scribbling on the move. As long as CJ got a daily telegraphed report filled with trivia about sleeves, shawls, collars, or hat trimmings in vogue with the English aristocracy wintering in Egypt, he need never know she had flagrantly ignored almost every other of his copious instructions.

Today at last he wanted more than the trend in neckwear, and it was all here in her notebooks. She leafed through pages of scribbled notes and sketches of ornate millinery to find the entry titled, in tall, firm printing, "Eccentric Adventurer Exits Egypt."

"TD, do we have any images of the baron's departure?"

The sparrow's brass wings shimmered in a beam of sunlight as he flapped to the desk. He tapped the inkwell with his beak until she reached over to open the lid. His throat buzzed softly as he drank. Then he hopped over to the blotter where she laid out a fresh sheet of paper and secured its corners with pins. When he began to dot-dash lines onto the page, she turned back to her notebook, scribbling on a separate sheet. At the end of the page, she stopped writing and read over what she had written, crossing out a word here and inserting another there.

"The eccentric English adventurer, Baron Bodmin, left Cairo early this year on a dangerous quest for a legendary treasure known as the Eye of Africa.

A large white stone with veins of red in its heart, the so-called "Bloodshot Diamond" was reportedly set in a tribal mask as a third eye. Nubian legend says the diamond lights up with a fantastical red glow if touched by an evildoer's blood. The baron widely claimed he possessed secret knowledge to lead him to the mask's hiding place, an uncharted oasis deep in the Nubian desert.

During the long refit of his expeditionary airship, the Jules Verne, *for desert travel, Baron Bodmin was best known in Cairo for elegant dinner parties at Shepheard's English Hotel. On January fifth of this year, he set out from Cairo aerodrome at dusk and never returned.*

The baron's fate remains unknown. Was his quest fruitless? Were his bones picked clean by hungry desert-denizens? How came his ship to be floating, unattended, so far from Egypt? Could it, indeed, have traversed the Mediterranean Sea and all Europe un-guided by a human hand? If there is a clue to his fate in Egypt, your faithful correspondent will excavate it and report it here, in the pages of . . ."

She left the name of the newspaper blank. Let CJ decide where to place her prose to best effect. The sparrow's pattering over his page petered out with a final dot-dot-dot, and she looked at the picture he had produced: the baron at the aerodrome, lit by the setting sun as he leaned toward a beautiful, dark-haired woman.

"Oh, yes, that soldier's widow." Maddie wiped the little bird's beak free of ink. "The blue evening gown with bouffant sleeves and the adventurous neckline so suitable for displaying jewels. I wonder if she hung onto that diamond-and-sapphire collar the baron gave her, or if he demanded it back. He seemed that kind of man. But I expect she's acquired another protector by now."

This style of remark had given Mother the vapours on Maddie's last, incognito visit to London, but Maddie was not the sheltered debutante who had fled her own ball two years earlier. She knew men and women formed irregular connections that did not lead to marriage. Similar connections had been offered to Maddie on her travels, in token of her youth and lack of looming male relatives, but thus far she had not accepted any offers. Or jewels.

"I must find out where the widow went," she told the bird, "and gain an interview. She is, after all, the last person known to have spoken to the baron before he vanished." She transcribed her article onto a telegraph sheet, using the much-condensed word forms beloved of penny-pinching newspapers editors, and hoped whoever expanded them at the other end did so correctly. Wiping a splotch of ink from one dainty finger, she re-fixed her hat and donned a clean pair of gloves. Someone in the tea-and-gossip party that was Shepheard's English Hotel would know the fair widow's name and direction. "Wait here, TD, while I send this telegraph and pursue my inquiries."

The little bird gave a small warble that might have been disapproval, but hopped to his windowsill and resumed staring out at swallows and pigeons, and the Egyptian hawks that circled lazily above the teeming city of mud-brick and stone, occasionally swooping down to prey on the smaller birds.

In early April, Shepheard's remained filled with British winter residents, most of whom were gathered in the tea-garden at this hour. After sending her telegram to CJ, Maddie paused in the archway, scanning for likely gossips among the sea of pastel muslin tea dresses. Pale plastered walls reflected murmuring voices and the whisper of water from several fountains. Potted palms rustled as fans whirred in the vaulting overhead, driven by a complex array of rods and gears. Arches along the far wall opened the tearoom to the courtyard, where stately palms augmented the shade of the massive hotel's wings. Wicker tables draped in pristine linen were dotted across the ochre floor tiles. Running among them were self-propelling tea-carts, dispensing the genial beverage with puffs of steam. Waiters bore trays of dainties and pitchers of cream. Ruffled and ribbon-strewn ladies at every table paused in the act of lifting teacups or plying fans, hoping the eye of the young lady reporter would light upon their Indian shawls or Irish lace cuffs.

At last Maddie spotted the pastel peach hat trimmings of the hotel's longest resident, Lady Hartington-Holmes. Her nieces, both destined for the next London Season, were visiting to acquire social polish. As every mention in a Society page enhanced their luster back home, in which effort Maddie had often obliged—although to be frank she could not tell one girl from the other—she had no qualms about approaching the group uninvited. Conveniently, Lady HH was already discussing the morning's news about Baron Bodmin, specifically his penchant for purchasing jewelry for "that woman." Maddie accepted a teacup from one niece and a cream cake from another, and raised an eyebrow.

The niece in blue tittered. "That dashing widow!"

"If she was a widow," the other niece added, as pink as her gauzy shawl.

Blue nodded. "Colonel Muster told me she was . . ."

"Ahem." Lady HH cleared her throat and the girl fell silent. "Yes, that widow," said the elder woman with distaste. "Her husband, she said, was an officer in the Fifth, lost on a desert campaign. This visit was in the nature of a pilgrimage, she said. Hah. A hunting expedition, more like. She arrived not long after the baron, and if they were not acquainted before, she lost no time in drawing him like a bee to a blossom. Men. Hah." She paused to refresh her throat with tea. "No woman of standing accepts diamonds from a man she is neither related to nor expecting to marry."

genial beverage

Maddie raised the other eyebrow.

"Yes, diamonds," said the blue niece. "A full set. The necklace, bracelets, earrings. No ring, though, and you know what that means."

"She wasn't offered marriage," the pink niece clarified, her cheeks glowing with the lure of illicit romance.

"And this colonel told you something about her marriage?"

Lady HH huffed loudly. "I learned, eventually, that no officer in the Fifth had ever borne that name. But Colonel Muster did not think fit to inform *me* of the impersonation." She glared at the blue niece, who apparently had not informed her either.

"Such a lovely party for the baron's farewell," said the pink niece, with the clear aim of changing the subject.

"You attended, did you not, Miss Hatter?" added the blue niece.

"I did," said Maddie. "And I went to the aerodrome to watch the baron's airship lift off."

"Aunt would not allow us," said the pink niece. "Was it terribly exciting, with the sun setting and the banners streaming? The Cairo newssheets all had the same image, blurry and gray, with the mooring lines still attached."

"Not that exciting. No banners nor a speech of parting. More a sense of a dangerous venture about to begin." Maddie paused. "The widow was with him at the aerodrome."

The nieces turned rapt faces to her. "Did she faint?" asked one. "Did she depart with him?" asked the other.

"She wept, from what I could tell," said Maddie. TD's picture had helped her recollect the moment: the dainty woman a scant few years older than herself, weeping as the setting sun snagged on the diamonds at her wrist. "I watched the baron board the *Jules Verne*, alone, and he drew up the gangplank immediately. I never saw her after that moment either, although she had been occupying a room along my corridor for weeks."

"We quite thought she had gone with him," said Lady HH, "without benefit of matrimony."

"Perhaps she followed her lover across the desert on a horse," said the blue niece. "Or hid herself amongst a camel caravan."

"If she was lost to savages in the desert," said the pink, "it is a harsher fate than she deserved for flaunting a few diamonds."

Lady HH glared down the nieces, but ladies at nearby tables were quick to add their iota about the faux widow. Some opined that being torn apart by savages was just what a certain class of woman deserved, and others declared there was no proof the so-called widow had been immoral, only that the baron wished to make her so.

Eventually Maddie tired of trying to winkle out details that might lead to the mysterious widow's present name or whereabouts, and retired to the lobby. She looked around the vast, hexagonal space, hoping to snaffle a few male guests with quotable opinions of the baron's quest. The Moorish archway and colourful architectural flourishes had ceased to dazzle months ago, and the immensely high ceiling left her merely grateful that the inevitable heat of a Cairo springtime afternoon had room to rise.

Brass messenger tracks wove almost invisibly through the patterned tiles on the walls unless, as now, one of the flat note-cases, no larger around than the palm of her hand, went crawling up, down, or across a wall before her eyes. A falcon head engraving meant a destination in the Horus wing, but the disc was a bit too far away to make out the little room-number calibrator. Not that it would be for her anyway. She was in the Bast wing at the rear of the hotel, where the Egyptians and their British overlords considered both female deities and living females belonged. If she'd known the baron would disappear in mysterious circumstances, she would have cultivated an acquaintance among the message-transcription staff, and learned of messages sent to or from the baron. Did the hotel keep copies of guest messages? Perhaps she should inquire, pretending to have lost one of hers.

Meanwhile, she scanned the lobby again for any sign of an eminent male who might grant her a word on the record. But it was the wrong time of day for accosting gentlemen. Most were gathered in the smoking room over their brandy, discussing the latest news from London. She needed the latest news too. If the baron was already discovered in England, there would be no point pursuing the story in Cairo, and she would have to wait for another chance to prove herself worthy of a byline.

Leaning over a nearby table, she placed a penny in the paw of the brass monkey seated there, and spun him to face her. The creature's forearm ratcheted upward to deposit the coin in his mouth. He rolled to her edge of the table. After a few clicks and wheezes, his vest-front opened up, revealing a small screen on which scrolled miniscule editions of the London daily news. She twisted his little brass buttons, slowing the feed enough to read the headlines, and pumped his other arm to increase the size of the type-face whenever the baron's name appeared.

There was nothing new except that the baron's nephew was on his way to Cairo to make inquiries. He had, it appeared, only learned of his uncle's disappearance on being accosted by a reporter outside a Parisian gaming house. Perhaps she could nab him for an interview, although, if he was traveling overland as the article indicated, he could not arrive for at least a week. She made a note of his name—Sir Ambrose Peacock—and scrolled on.

When her eyes crossed from the strain of squinting, she poked the monkey's nose to send it rolling back to its place. No gentlemen had yet strolled by, ready to be snared for a quote, and she did not quite dare to penetrate entirely male sanctums like the smoking room. She would have to try again after the evening meal.

As she was tucking away her notebook, a prosperous merchant strode in. Silken robes and embroidered vests wafted about him, releasing clouds of exotic scent. A clerk scuttled in his wake. The merchant slammed a rolled paper onto the main desk, shouting at the startled manager in fast, incomprehensible Egyptian, and slapped the countertop to punctuate his points. The manager protested, shaking his head and even, briefly, his fist. Much yelling ensued, but without apparent resolution. The merchant stalked out, robes flapping and clerk scuttling crablike after. The scroll stayed on the polished wood of the desk, the manager eying it like he might an asp.

That excitement over, Maddie made her way upstairs. As the ascender wheezed and creaked its way upward, she asked its steward what the fuss at the desk had been about. This fellow, often a recipient of minor baksheesh for explaining Egypt to her, had no hesitation in telling all he knew.

"The jewels, young Sitt. Diamonds and other gems, bought by the English baron who was lost in his airship. He had them here to decide which to buy, and left before sending them back. The jewel merchant is not paid, and now he knows the baron is not coming back, he is angry. The hotel is not paid for the baron's rooms, and is angry. The lady who was supposed to pay has said she will not pay. Not for the baron's rooms, nor the baron's parties, nor the jewels." He scratched one ear where his fez had rubbed it. "She is angry too, I think."

"This lady who was to pay, was she staying at the hotel?" Could the tea gossips have had it so wrong, and the widow was supporting the baron instead of vice versa?

"No, young Sitt. That lady is far away in England. She has only the man at the bank to speak for her. The baron had papers to let him take money from the bank."

Not the widow, but another woman, in England, ensnared by the dashing adventurer. Maddie elicited the name of the bank and handed over a few modest coins, already mentally composing her next headline. Large-living baron bilks lonely lady? If someone could be brought to reveal her name, CJ could surely find the woman for a quote.

As she returned to her room along the quiet, second-class corridor, with its boring British box-shape and the message track with absolutely no ornamentation to disguise its brassy utility, Maddie once more pondered her new byline. It had to look good in 10-point type. Ah, well, she could remain "Our Cairo Correspondent" for one more article.

No portrait, though, not ever. Under the new deal, her parents could withhold her allowance if she were recognized while doing something so outrageous as earning a living. The allowance had paid her way to Egypt and, until the coin began to trickle in from fashion columns, had provided her shelter, her food, and the endless supply of white gloves that gave her dubious profession an air of respectability. If it stopped, her savings would barely get her back to England at the end of the current assignment, and CJ would not offer another post if the project lost her father's grudging favour. Nobody willingly offended a Steamlord, especially over a family matter.

She stepped into her utilitarian bedchamber and told TD, "Tomorrow I will wear my best suit and the hat with the ribbons that hide you best. We will infiltrate the bank, and then the jeweler. You must record any conversation at the first, and collect images at the second. A pictorial record of pilfered jewels will catch CJ's fancy no end."

Setting her notebook on the desk in preparation for an article on Indian-style parasols for Spring, she flipped up the lid on the inkwell and prepared to dip her pen. She paused, and thoughtfully rested her index finger on a faintly shiny bit of the carved walnut surround. One push and she would have her old visiting card back from the secret drawer. The Honourable Madeleine Main-Bearing, daughter of the Marquis of Main-Bearing, could command assistance from any official in the British Empire, and some beyond it. A mere bank manager would be as butter in the sun before that card. But there were only five, and if she carried them, she would be tempted to use them to smooth her path. Showing one would be tantamount to admitting she could not, in fact, make her way in the world alone. She would not admit that. Not yet. She pulled her finger away, picked up the pen, and began to write.

Chapter Two

WITHIN A VERY few minutes of walking into the bank, Maddie found herself returned to the street outside. The sun warmed a face positively chilled by polite refusals. On pretext of adjusting her hat, she touched TD's beak to stop him recording. The words spoken inside that edifice were not a shining example of investigative journalism anyway. She would have to do better, or resort to her family visiting card after all. Ah, well, the jewel merchant was only a street away, housed not in the medina in the street of the jewelers, but on a thoroughfare catering to Europeans. She would not approach him head-on.

In the jeweler's modern shop, after a rapid assessment of Maddie's two-year-old suit, a minor functionary came forward and asked, in impeccable English, how he might assist her.

"I do hope you can," she said. "My cousin is passing through Cairo soon, after his tour of the archaeological sites, and asked me to look for jewels suitable for his fiancée back in England. He saw something purchased by his old schoolmate, Baron

17

Bodmin, which he thought came from here. Do you have pieces that might interest him?" She watched the gears turn as the minion made the calculations: a gentleman of means, acquainted with an absconding baron but not claiming him as friend, who could afford a winter's tour in Egypt and wanted a gift suitable for an English woman of similar social standing. He bowed slightly and began to draw out velvet-lined trays.

"The baron, as I recall, was partial to the Nefertiti line, made by our finest smiths in honour of that most beloved consort." He expanded upon the jewels as he lifted them one by one from their trays: how the baron had chosen this style of golden brooch fixed with lapis and onyx, in the shape of the long-dead queen's official profile. Also a necklace like this one, mimicking the Nefertiti collar's bright hues in sapphires and diamonds.

Maddie reached up to hold her hat as she bent over the trays, and made many admiring noises. When the minion had worked his way through the collection she asked, for her cover story, to see a few pieces not related to Nefertiti, and came away almost certain that TD had captured images of very similar pieces to the missing jewels. She hurried back to the hotel, past the ladies gossiping on the terrace, and set the little bird on the desk next to the inkwell. If the widow in herself was not memorable, perhaps her jewels would help track her down. They would indubitably add allure to a newspaper article about her.

After a luncheon at which the same speculations were heard from the same ladies about the baron and the widow, Maddie started upstairs intending to compose an article about the missing jewels. Should she include the baron's financial finagling, or would that be risking a suit for libel? Best to inform CJ separately and let him decide. She made a mental note to seek out legal opinions on what constituted libel. This was never a problem when all she wrote was fashion commentary, but an investigative journalist needed to know what was fit to print.

Lady HH's pink niece caught up to her as she left the ascender. Huffing a bit from hurrying up the stairs in a ridiculously tight pink-and-cream corset, the niece leaned against the flocked wallpaper to regain her breath, and beckoned Maddie closer.

Maddie could not recall immediately which of the nieces this was. They both had the family last name, after all. "Do you require aid, er, Miss?"

"Clarice." Pink sucked in as deep a breath as her corset would allow. "My cousin is Nancy. Not that I expect you to remember, when you meet so many people in your work. Although you mentioned my Indian muslin hat trimmings particularly back in January. It was in a *Cornwall Cog & Goggles* column."

"Ah." Maddie nodded as if she remembered. "And you would like to bring a new trim to my attention?"

Pink—er, Clarice—shook her golden curls and looked toward the ascender. "I haven't much time before Nancy comes looking for me."

"Oh." Maddie glanced around the deserted corridor. "Would you care to step into my chamber?"

"Please!" Clarice followed her to the less exalted wing of the hotel. In the room she gazed around at the sturdy furniture without comment and seated herself at the little table only when invited to do so.

Maddie sat in the other straight-backed chair and opened her sequined notebook.

"You wanted to tell me something? About the mysterious, er, widow?"

Clarice bit her lip. "Could you tell me something first?"

"If I may." That was sufficiently vague, allowing Maddie to withhold information for any number of reasons.

"Is it true that Baron Bodmin's nephew, Sir Ambrose Peacock, is coming here? To Cairo?"

"It was mentioned in the aethernet news from London. Overland, so he won't arrive for several days at best."

The pink niece sighed. "I hoped you might have heard from your newspaper sources whether he is truly coming, for he cannot send me another message unless Colonel Muster comes back to Egypt."

"Colonel Muster, that friend of the baron's? What has he to do with Sir Ambrose?"

Clarice looked down at her hands. "The colonel brought me holiday greetings from Sir Ambrose at Christmas." The obvious question was why the baron's nephew was sending messages by an intermediary, but that was nothing to Maddie.

"If I hear anything particular about the nephew, I will tell you." Ignoring the girl's sigh, she set out Tweetle-D's images of the jeweled collar and the Nefertiti brooch. "Do you remember the jewels the mysterious widow was wearing? Were they like these?"

"Oh, yes, very like," said Clarice, after a glance. "Colonel Muster was very put out about the baron buying them."

"Your aunt did not wish Colonel Muster discussed yesterday?"

"Aunt disapproved of my talking aside with an older gentleman. Even a war hero like the colonel. She said the family would never allow me to throw myself away on a penniless ex-officer with tarnished medals. I did not quite understand what she meant, for his medals looked well-polished to me. But I could not say so, for he only took me aside to hand over a note and a little gift." Clarice's pink cheeks grew rosier. "From Sir Ambrose, that is. I dared not mention *him* to Aunt when she asked what the colonel wanted."

An illicit attachment to the baron's nephew? When had it developed? "Sir Ambrose must have left Egypt before I arrived."

"Oh, he did not come to Egypt at all. He hoped to when Father sent me here, but his uncle, the baron, would not pay his passage. He paid for the colonel to come out, and that funny professor who visited him over Christmas. So why not his own nephew and only heir?"

To that grievance there seemed no satisfactory answer. Maddie tried to draw Clarice back to exactly what the colonel had said of the widow, but the girl could not be swayed until she had told of her first meeting with Sir Ambrose at the British Museum, and their subsequent snatched moments, hand-pressings, and sweet compliments, finally finishing with her father's outrage when her little romance came to light. "He said horrible things about dear Ambrose's motives, and sent me all the way to Aunt in Egypt, where I am to remain until the start of the

London Season. So you see, I could scarce mention dear Sir Ambrose to Aunt when she asked what Colonel Muster wanted, because he was bringing me news of the man I was forbidden to see."

"Yes, I quite comprehend," said Maddie, suppressing an eye-roll. Clarice's tale was exactly the silly debutante chatter she had abandoned along with her old life. Two years made a vast difference in the preoccupations of a gently-raised girl. Especially when that two years was filled, as Maddie's had been, with far-ranging adventures and a vastly wider array of acquaintances than a peer's daughter would ever meet under normal circumstances.

"As soon as the baron is declared dead," Clarice continued, "Sir Ambrose will inherit his uncle's estate in Cornwall. I'm sure Father will let me speak to him then. But he hasn't yet approached Father and Aunt won't budge without Father's word. You must see how frustrating that is."

Having dodged her own family's plans for a suitable match, Maddie felt a pang of sympathy for the girl. Suppressing it, she asked for the third time, "And the colonel told you something about the widow?"

"Well, he knew for a fact there was no officer in that regiment by the name she claimed was her husband's."

That much Maddie had already learned. "Is that all?"

Clarice nodded, then shook her head. "Oh, and she snooped around the aerodrome trying to get aboard the baron's airship, before she was ever introduced to him. The baron took it to indicate she was interested in airships and adventures, and was even more besotted with her."

That was the sum of Clarice's knowledge. Easing the girl out of the room took a few minutes more, and a faithful promise never to divulge to Aunt or Papa that Sir Ambrose had sent her a billet-doux and a Christmas gift all the way to Cairo, while he was still poor and ineligible.

"Well, TD," said Maddie as she closed the door, "what has my initial investigation wrought? Only that the baron had a lady investor, whose money he spent lavishly, as well as a poor nephew in England, a mysterious mistress in Cairo, and, oh, yes, his two friends who were here at Christmas. Colonel Muster and that professor. What do I know about them?"

As she settled for her pre-prandial rest, Maddie let her mind drift back to the British Christmas festivities.

She had reached Cairo in mid-December, stepping off the Nile steamship's gangplank to the exotic wail of Egyptian reed flutes. After a time, she recognized the tune the street musicians strove toward: O Tannenbaum. It had been a chilly, overland journey through the winter rains from England to Venice by train, and then on a steamship from Venice. An airship would have arrived in half the time and been considerably more comfortable, but even a second-class air passage cost twice as much as surface travel.

At Shepheard's Hotel, she'd faced less risk of recognition than she'd feared for her first time back amongst the society she'd fled two years earlier. No more that delicate blossom of English girlhood, her facial features all but eclipsed by the rat-padded, over-curled coiffeur in the signature bronze locks of the Main-Bearings. The hair had been the first thing to go, the bottom half hacked off in a Euston Station powder room and the rest painted a hasty brown, scraped into a practical chignon. Her fair skin was weather-kissed now in a way that would seriously distress her mother, but back then she had merely wiped away the expensive cosmetics to have a face as commonplace as any working girl's. She could also rely upon the nobility's notorious inability to see the faces of the lower classes. Nobody who mattered recognized the dainty daughter of a peer behind the ink-splashed notebook of a hard-working lady journalist, because they were not looking for one.

Arriving in the heart of Cairo, Maddie found the December air not warmer than an English summer day, but so dry it stuck in her throat, and scented exotically, although not always pleasantly, with spices and sweating humans. An open space along the river was crowded with cargo, camels, and harried officials. She followed her porter and her trunk past a line of self-propelling carriages and traversed a wide avenue filled with carts and camels. Beggars dogged her for a few steps before abandoning her for travelers more ostentatiously dressed.

They came almost at once to Shepheard's English Hotel. The multi-story stone building with its boxy windows and iron railings would not have looked out of place in London. In Egypt it was a monstrous imposition over the low brick buildings and wooden lattices built by the native population. The porter hauled the trunk up shallow, stone steps. Maddie followed, conscious of the dust on her clothing as immaculately turned-out coffee drinkers on

Shepheard's famous terrace openly stared at her. Inside, the lobby was a vast Moorish fantasyland. Its walls were pierced by tall, pointed arches of coloured limestone. Pilasters, niches, and faux lintels rose to the elaborately corniced ceiling. Her trunk was taken over by an automaton painted to look like an English footman, and she was escorted upstairs by a British matron in a widow's cap, whose pinched look told all the world her opinion of young ladies who traveled alone.

The dining room she saw that first luncheon was another Moorish vastness, with tile decorating the walls, arches, and niches. Immense columns called to mind lithographs of ancient temples. These columns, however, were painted in bright hues no aquatint artist could hope to reproduce. How could she tear her eyes from this magnificence to make notes on the quite ordinary lace and muslin fashions on the ladies present? But record fashion she must if she wished to earn her way, and so she took notes while giving her fictional biography to the gossipy English ladies at her table, and hearing all of theirs at quite tedious length.

Seasonal festivities began the very next day with an air-land parade, a custom borrowed from the grand parades in London and New York City. She followed the other guests up to the rooftop patio, where chairs had been arranged for them along the parapet, with a good view of the sky above and the street below. Parasols blossomed over all the ladies, even those with hats larger than a tea tray. Maddie, unable to hold a parasol while recording notes by hand, had opted for her widest hat, trimmed with metallic ribbon in which TD could pass for mere ornamentation while recording images for later transmission to London. She took a chair slightly back from the first rank and jotted brief impressions of typical English attire as adapted to the hot, dry, climate of the desert city.

Very little adaptation, was her first observation: several layers were worn by both ladies and gentlemen, jackets over waistcoats over shirts with long sleeves, tight cuffs, and high necks. Already uncomfortably warm in her thinnest summer garments from England, she foresaw that her small store of money must be further depleted by the purchase of less restrictive clothing.

The first strains of a marching band drifted up on the arid breeze. A Highland regiment came swinging along the street just as it would at home, except for the dust that rose up from fifty sets of pounding feet and rolled in an ochre wave over the hotel terrace. Now the wisdom of watching from the rooftop was plain. In London, in December, dust was never a problem.

In London, the parade would be enlivened by airships carrying burghers of the City's guilds, floating along in the first traffic tier above the street, their slender gondolas brightly disguised as scarlet sleighs, gilded carriages, and gift-wrapped boxes. Here a string of dusty military scout-ships took their place, sand-blasted hulls and rigging strung with Union Jack bunting. The airships were followed by the Cairo Police precision heli-cycle team, whose flying was far from precise. Never would a formation flying team back home allow their group banner to sag between cycles, much less droop low enough to brush a camel's head, as the Cairene police team managed to do almost at the steps of Shepheard's.

In fairness, there were not often camels on London streets. This camel bit its neighbour, precipitating a skirmish. Handlers, their dusty robes flapping, yelled commands and curses. A donkey caught a kick and scattered its load of brass vessels across the road. Clashing and crashing sent the English officers' horses dancing. Ah, Egypt. Maddie tilted her head to let TD capture images that would surely gladden even the ink-black heart of CJ Kettle.

There was one elaborate airship, at the far end of the parade. By the time it reached the hotel, the dust from the street had risen to the second floor. Maddie spared a thought for the bedchambers there—were the high windows securely closed? Then the airship was abreast, its name spelled out in bright scrollwork along the gondola's fore-quarters: *Jules Verne*.

The *Jules Verne* was long and lean, its outer gondola sheathed in what looked like dark walnut wood, newly polished. Brass fittings and metallic envelope dazzled in the mid-day sun. Streamers outlined its panoramic windows. A Union Jack flew under the keel. Through wide-open cockpit windows, a man in a morning coat tipped his gleaming white pith helmet toward the hotel roof.

A matron in the first row waved a handkerchief and called out, "Hello, Baron," and a scholarly gentleman nearby cried out, "Well done, sir."

As the airship passed, a cable became visible, attached at the stern and rising high into the sky. Maddie followed it upward, one hand shielding her eyes. Far above, unmoving against the stark, blue dome, was a military scouting balloon. As she watched, something fell from it, black and scarlet tumbling through the sky, taking on the unmistakable shape of a man's body.

Others saw it too, gasping and pointing as it hurtled ever earthward. A girl shrieked. Another slid from her chair in a dead faint.

Just when it seemed the man must crash to earth and be crushed by his own momentum, the scarlet billowed outward, becoming a vast canopy that caught the air and arrested the plunge.

Jerked suddenly upright, the aeronaut tugged at a cord, turning the canopy toward the hotel, and waved to the pointing throng. They scattered as he came on. Servants and gentlemen dragged chairs from the center of the flat roof, and there he landed, neatly on his feet. The scarlet canopy settled behind him, looking, thought Maddie, like a pool of wet blood across the dusty tiles. The daring aeronaut brushed off his black flying suit and bowed to his gaping audience.

"Who is that man?" Maddie asked a girl at her side.

"Colonel Muster," said the girl, wide-eyed and flushed in her long-sleeved, cream-lace and primrose frock. "He is a war hero, newly come from England to visit the man who owns that lovely airship. Baron Bodmin. Have you met him yet?"

"Not yet. I too am newly from England. Mad—" she caught herself. "Maddie Hatter. Fashion correspondent for the Kettle Conglomerate."

From that second Sunday in Advent, the English residents' evenings were enlivened by merry parlour games and frequent lusty singing of carols. Archaeological staff returned from their excavations. The celebrated Egyptologist, Mr. Petrie, arrived to general acclaim and a reserved suite in a first-class corridor. A close relation of Her Majesty took up residence in the Royal Suite that opened onto the balcony over the famous terrace; he promptly complained of the noise from below and was moved to an almost equally opulent suite overlooking the hotel's courtyard garden. Sometime amongst all the other arrivals, the beautiful, young, self-proclaimed widow took up residence next door to Maddie. She effortlessly attracted the attention of all the males in her vicinity, much to the chagrin of the nieces in pink and blue, who had, until that point, been enjoying rather a lot of mild flirtation.

The hotel's little orchestra played Christmas music at every possible occasion, until Maddie began to prowl the streets around the hotel, ever surrounded by loudly begging children, just to escape from the relentless tunes. The British baron and his war-hero guest were present at every festivity. The former was fond of talking about his quest for a fabulous treasure. Maddie tried in vain to interest CJ in a serial story of his proposed adventure. Surely expeditions in search of legendary treasures would interest readers more than the exact style of ascot the royal relation had worn this week?

The dashing colonel wore dark spectacles indoors and out, lending him an air of mystery, and not a little danger. He claimed his eyes were weakened by too many years staring into the sun at high altitude. Young men grumbled that the specs gave him an advantage at the card table, since he could read their expressions easily while his was half concealed. Lady HH told the ladies over tea one day that young Viscount S— had lost so extensively to the colonel that his father had to come in person to Cairo, to pay his bills and take him ignominiously away. Flush with winnings or not, Colonel Muster continued his gaming unabated, except when he was closeted with the baron over decanters, airship schematics, and vague charts of the desert.

On Christmas Eve, Baron Bodmin threw a lavish dinner party. He had caused real fir trees to be flown in from somewhere, and they blazed with real candles beside every pillar in the vast dining room, dripping wax into their sand-filled tubs and onto the floor tiles. The tables were dressed with holly and ivy and fat, red candles. A sumptuous feast of roast turkey, pan gravy, and all the traditional side dishes was brought in by the steam-driven serving carts, each one attended by a human server to pile high the pre-warmed plates. This was followed by flaming puddings with the appropriate sauces. A heavy meal indeed in the summery climate.

When the first guests had pushed back their chairs, preparing to slip away, Baron Bodmin rose and held up his hands for attention.

"Friends," he said. "You've all met my good friend, Colonel Muster, who is a crucial supporter of my work in so many ways. Today I proudly introduce to you my other great supporter, an erudite Professor of Ancient Civilizations from Cambridge, Professor Polonius Plumb, whose research into the Nubian tribes is at the heart of my quest." The man seated beside him stood up, resplendent in an oriental silk smoking gown quite unsuitable for a mixed dinner party. Unlike the baron and the colonel, his physique was not that of a man of action, but rather academically round-shouldered, and with a slight rounding of the mid-section as well. He began to speak, but the baron cut him off with a reminder of the ball about to start.

Later, as the ballroom in turn heated up under the influence of its dazzling chandeliers and a horde of energetic young men dancing non-stop with the first young ladies they'd seen in three long desert months, Maddie slipped out to the courtyard to cool her flushed cheeks under the vast midnight sky. She was seated in a wicker chair, deep in shadow by the library windows, gazing up at the stars, when she heard the baron's voice again. It came from inside the library.

"No, I will not advance you more money. I paid your way out here, didn't I?"

An unfamiliar voice replied. "If it were not for me, you wouldn't have the money to pay your own way. I got you everything you needed to convince that woman to back you. And how much are you giving that leech, Muster? He'll bleed your estate dry while you're gone."

"It won't matter. I'll have the Eye and you'll have the story of a lifetime."

"As long as Jones doesn't find out. If he makes a fuss, I'll lose everything." The professor—for so Maddie had later identified the peevish voice—had gone on talking until someone else entered the room. Had he spoken the wealthy investor's name?

More than three months later, stifling in the April afternoon's considerable warmth, Maddie sat up on her bed. The investor's name might be in her notebook from that night. That would be a coup for CJ. She could spin out an article, too, about the colonel and the professor advising on the expedition, leaving it to reporters back home to get quotes from them. She swept aside the mosquito netting that surrounded her mattress and set about digging back through her stack of notebooks for the sunny yellow one, labeled *Cornwall Cog and Goggles*. It had seemed a fitting choice when the gray skies of Europe gave way to brilliantly sunny African skies on the Mediterranean crossing.

She had been so enthusiastic about her completely independent job at first that the whole notebook filled up by Christmas. And there it was on the last page, the professor's angry tirade as best she could remember it. He had not mentioned the investor by name, merely cautioned that Baron Bodmin had better bring back that mask or she would be very angry with him. "She." The wealthy investor was a woman, but what was her name?

If Maddie recalled aright, the professor and Colonel Muster had both left for England directly after the New Year. Someone in England would have to follow up.

The safragi came along the corridor then, tapping on doors to warn that teatime approached. While pinning up her hair afresh, Maddie considered what might have gone wrong with the expeditionary airship. Had the baron skimped on setting up his actual expedition, and some oversight led to his eventual downfall?

"What a pity," she told TD, who was looking on from the top of the armoire, "what a pity we don't know anyone in Cornwall, who could send us a detailed description of that airship's present condition. But perhaps someone in Cairo was aboard before it left here. How would I find such a person?"

The widow, or whatever she really was. She had been nosing around the aerodrome, asking questions about the baron's airship before she moved to the hotel. She may have known if it was not desert-worthy. She might be remembered at the aerodrome even now, for workmen the world over took good note of a beautiful woman. In any event, the workers there were Maddie's best, and possibly final, chance of getting quotes from anyone knowledgeable about the airship. Did it have the right supplies and equipment to keep a man alive for three months in the desert? Tomorrow's target: the aerodrome.

The next thought struck her with such force that she dropped her hairbrush. "What if he's not dead? What if he intended all along to vanish if he found the mask? What a coup that would be, if we were to find out he's alive after all."

Chapter Three

STANDING BEFORE THE Concierge Desk, Maddie mentally counted her coins while the attendant awaited her decision. She had not arrived by air and not realized the distance or cost involved in reaching the aerodrome. For the baron's departure, the hotel had laid on steam-driven omnibuses. Surrounded by a chattering crowd of well-wishers and taking copious notes about the adventure—which CJ ignored—she had not found the drive long. Now she discovered a full hour's travel each way by self-propelling carriage would cost as much as a day's lodging. The alternative was a donkey cart, which took twice as long for a third of the price. If she did not wish to be caught out in the baking pinnacle of afternoon, which might be dangerous to one wearing a navy blue wool suit with the shady, but weighty, TD-carrying hat, the greater cost must be borne. She signed the charge slip and left the attendant to make arrangements.

She set off soon after breakfast, with the carriage's sunshade retracted that she might better enjoy the sights of the city. The driver, his white robe and turban spotless, sat up on his bench swinging his steering bar wildly, yelling at other drivers, and telling her in rapid, idiomatic English about the Ismailia Square (which was round) and other noteworthy features they passed. Arches, minarets, and upper-story balconies screened by elegant latticework gave way gradually to smaller, squarer, flat-roofed buildings with low parapets. Some of these modest quarters were enlivened by tiled arches, through which she glimpsed courtyards paved with ancient, intricate mosaic. Other walls were old stone, patched with flaking plaster or shored up by rough timbers. There were stretches of desert too, among the settled areas, and soon the houses barely lined the one road, with only sand and date palms beyond. Had her driver taken her a roundabout way?

The aerodrome's direction was confirmed when a massive shadow floated between her and the sun. She tipped her head far back, dislodging TD. Overhead, an international liner was passing, hundreds of feet long, with the crest of the White Sky Line in brass on its underbelly. The line, she knew, was American, but its luxurious airships flew many routes over Europe as well as across the ocean. It sailed low over the rooftops, with passengers crowding the open deck to point and exclaim over the exotic sights below. Other, smaller ships filled the sky around it, arriving and departing in many directions. Soon moored ships were visible too, bobbing close to the sand while bales and crates were carried on and off by natives in ragged robes. Almost there!

She began to seriously consider who to approach, and how. After tipping her driver she paused, watching the White Sky craft's final descent, ground crews hauling on the dangling lines until they could be hitched to steam winches fore and aft. The great ship settled alongside the upper floor of the solidly British stone terminal building. Possibly Sir Ambrose was on that ship, if he had found the money for the fare. But was an interview with him worth more than learning the condition of the baron's airship at departure? She hurried instead to the nearest huge hangar. Blinking in the dim, she gazed up at a half-dozen military dirigibles that floated at anchor, their envelopes filling the vast space, and then snared the first workman she saw.

"I am looking for the men who refitted that expeditionary airship, the *Jules Verne,* last winter."

The man looked her over. "And who are you to be asking?"

"A journalist for the Kettle Conglomerate. I'm following up on that aeronaut who disappeared, and was told this facility outfitted the *Jules Verne* for desert travel. My readers back in London would like to know what's all involved in such a re-fit."

"Heard about that ship. Nothing to do with us, mind. That ship was in full working order when she left us."

"She was still in working order when she was found months later," said Maddie. "Thousands of miles over deserts, seas, and mountains, and still working. That's no bad reflection on the workmen."

"In that case, second hanger down on the left."

Maddie thanked him and hurried away. The second hanger was smaller, holding a handful of private airships bobbing from tethers while men in coveralls milled about them with tools and fuel lines. High up in the shadows, flocks of small birds swooped, scooping up insects. TD whistled to them. She shushed him with a touch and followed a steam-cart deep inside. A scrawny Egyptian pushed past with a large basket on one shoulder. Stepping back, she teetered as her boot came down on a thick cable.

"Steady on, miss," came an English voice from behind her. A hand gripped her elbow. "All right there?"

"Yes, thank you." She regained her balance and smiled at the man.

He smiled back. "Tricky footing in here unless you're used to it. Which you ain't. Help you find sommat?"

"I'm a journalist from England, looking for men who worked on an expeditionary airship last winter. My readers are interested in how a desert refit differs from an ordinary refit."

"That'd be the *Jules Verne*?" She nodded. "Sure and I was on the job meself," he added. "Ask away."

Through asking as many questions about airship workings as she could think of, Maddie was soon in the midst of a small cluster of men, all eager to impress the young lady reporter with their knowledge of gears, ballast, weight-to-envelope ratio, and the trials of sand-proofing an air-cooled engine for desert travel.

After carefully noting their answers, she said, "I suppose, since his life depended on the ship, the owner was here quite a lot to supervise. Was he difficult to deal with?"

"Not him," said her first friend. "Knew what he wanted done, and noticed good work. Open-handed too. Stood us all a pint every Friday."

"That's as may be," said another worker. "But he never paid his shot here, did he? Up and left, saying as how that lady's bank would pay. But it wouldn't. Lucky we got our wages by the week or we'd be out all that labour."

"The lady?"

"His investor. Owns the White Sky Line, I hear."

"Daughter of the feller what started it," said an older man. "Old White was canny with his coin, but her purse is closed tight as a new rivet."

Ah. The baron's lady investor. With this information, tracking her down would be a simple matter for CJ. Now, what about the other lady in the case? Maddie unfolded the image TD had made of the mysterious widow.

"Did this lady ever come to see the airship with the baron?"

Someone said, "I mind her. Not with the baron, but she were around a lot early on. Knew almost as much about airships as you do."

"That little?" Maddie laughed, and the men grinned.

"Now, miss, I'll allow you know the stem from the stern all right," said her friend. "That one, she asked a lot of questions too, but we never did find out what for, did we, lads?" They shook their heads and, as a foreman appeared around the hull of a ship, hurried back to their tasks.

Soon Maddie was alone in the cavernous hangar.

As she turned toward the sunshine beyond the huge doors, a sparrow darted past her head. So close was it in size and shape to TD that she put up her hand to ensure he was in his place. He whistled, and the sparrow zipped by a second time. Maddie ducked and hurried outside, and only then realized that, despite its resemblance to a real sparrow, this one might be another of the rare birds made by the mysterious corporation from which her old mentor had acquired TD. Did Madame Taxus-Hemlock's family conglomerate have an interest in the Cairo aerodrome, or did the owner of that bird come in on one of those ships? Maybe it was her particular friend, Oberon O'Reilly, her willing pal in so many adventures. She peered back into the dim, but saw nobody familiar. Ah, well, if Obie was nigh, he would make his presence known if he could. For now, work came first.

After savouring her unexpected lead on the baron's investor, she realized she had not asked about the widow's name. Who else might know? Surely the woman had paused for refreshment during her explorations, since the aerodrome was such a long way from the city proper. Maddie strolled off toward the imposing terminal and was soon seated in a tearoom of the most English kind, with white linen on the tables, sparkling cutlery, spotless teacups, and the ever-popular self-propelling beverage carts. The place was staffed by English too, both waiters and young ladies, who brought out dainty pastries and offered menus for those seeking heartier fare. Maddie chose a honey-drenched palace bread to accompany her thick, strong coffee, removed her net gloves, and looked around for anyone likely to be useful or quotable. To her great delight, she spotted a young naval officer who had come to many entertainments at Shepheard's. She raised a hand as his eyes swept the room. He hurried over.

"Miss Hatter, isn't it?" He bowed.

Maddie smiled. "It is. Stanislaus Swithin, is it not?"

"At your service. Do not say you are departing?"

"I'm not leaving Cairo yet," Maddie assured him. "Although, with the days growing ever hotter . . ."

"You are fortunate to have the option. I will be posted here until September. May I join you?"

"Please do." While he seated himself and waved for a waiter, she pulled out the image of the widow again. Leaving it face down on the table for the moment, she said, "I am writing an article on what is needed to fit out an airship for desert travel. This interest is inspired, as you may surmise, by the mystery of the *Jules Verne*, that flew thousands of miles since its refit here in Cairo. Could it have survived across the desert without a pilot?"

"Not across the desert, in the springtime, with the prevailing winds. Beyond that, I cannot see how it would end up in England without a steady hand on the tiller. There are all those Alps in the way, you know, and gales over the Mediterranean and the English Channel. No aeronaut would believe it."

"Then you think the baron must have been steering his ship most of the way?"

"Or someone was." The young officer ordered a hearty snack and collected his coffee from the cart that paused by their table. This was a most elegant machine, brass with chased silver knobs, although as loud in its explosion of steam through the grounds as any other machine of similar function. He turned the crank to add a foam of milk and sent the cart on its way.

"The baron's fate has the whole mess-hall in fervent debate. Some say he must have been taken by air pirates over the Sahara, while others point to his frequent mentions of Nubian treasure as proof he was going the other way. Yet, if the ship were pirate-taken, why go to England at all? The chance of being hailed for an identity check over Europe was great, and the winds weren't right to circle the ship out over the Atlantic instead. No, there is some greater mystery here. Oh, I say," he added as she flipped open her notebook. "Don't put me on the record. I'm not authorized."

"That's too bad." Maddie smiled at him. "You have been more quotable than anyone else I've spoken to here. I don't suppose you could direct me to someone who is authorized to speak?"

"I'll introduce you to my commander, if you will permit me."

"Delighted." After a short burst of social nothings, Maddie turned over the image. "I've been looking for this woman for a quote too. She was friendly with the baron. But I don't recall her name, and didn't ask where she was going when she moved from Shepheard's. I don't even know if she's still in Cairo."

The officer glanced at the image. "Oh, yes, her. She booked through to Venice in early February. I remember because the base admiral was most shocked that a Steamlord's daughter was traveling alone, and expedited matters to get her onto the next liner bound for Europe. Nobody wants to wear the stigma of losing somebody's daughter. Of course, you're somebody's daughter too, but your father's not a Steamlord kind of somebody. The Navy won't sail close to that breeze if we can help it. The Admiralty is almost totally dependent on Steamlord technology nowadays, and it wouldn't do to anger one of them."

Maddie didn't bother wondering why a Steamlord's daughter had lived in Cairo under an assumed name. She was doing it herself. She had not recognized the widow, but had they ever met, at school or in a drawing room? Had a kindred spirit lurked under a meek demeanor and a head of family-hued hair?

"What's her name? I could write to her care of her family."

"The Honourable Madeleine Main-Bearing, daughter of the Marquis of Main-Bearing."

Maddie dropped her cup.

Chapter Four

THE EARLY-AFTERNOON streets were somnolent as Maddie returned from the aerodrome. Her driver seemed half-asleep too; she poked him in the back with her pen whenever the vehicle strayed. In stark contrast to the earlier cacophony of camel and horse hooves, steam-whistles, and the eternal cries of sellers and beggars, now the rattle of the wheels and the intermittent hiss of the carriage's boiler were her only accompaniment. Minarets and screens, delicate mosaics, and carpets left hanging out in the sun to "antique" for the tourist trade, all passed her by unseen. The narrow roadways were stifling, with no breeze to flap the sunshade above her head or cool the fury in her veins.

The devious widow had parlayed one of Maddie's visiting cards into an escape from Egypt. Not only had that woman been inside Maddie's chamber uninvited, she had snooped very thoroughly indeed.

Worse still, she was long gone to Venice under Maddie's name, creating who knew what destruction to Maddie's reputation. If Lord Main-Bearing heard rumour that his daughter had been carousing publicly during Carnivale, she could not only lose her allowance but be air-dropped into a nunnery on a remote island off Scotland.

Maddie's best hope for discovering the extent of any damage was that second, possibly brass bird in the hangar. Its presence implied someone in Madame Taxus-Hemlock's immense family conglomerate had an interest in Cairo, and that meant their long-range birds would be circling the skies. If one of them passed within reach of the hotel, TD would know. At dark, he could be sent aloft to pass along a message. Madame's family—it was acknowledged by governments in several countries—had more spies in more places than any European power. For them, finding one woman using Maddie's name in Venice would be as easy as pouring a cup of tea.

Further, if anyone could advise Maddie on how to retrieve her reputation, track down the nefarious card-thief, and mitigate any parental ire, it would be Madame Taxus-Hemlock. She had seen everything and been everywhere, and, being a distant relative of the queen, could, in a pinch, over-awe Lord Main-Bearing into showing mercy to his daughter. Yes, the sooner Madame was informed of the imposter, the better. Still, Maddie seethed all the way to the hotel. If she ever caught up to that woman . . .

Maddie had barely flung her hat at her writing table when a hawk landed on her windowsill. It looked real but TD leapt to meet it, his little beak tapping at the glass. The hawk, its brass pinions cunningly painted to resemble a common Egyptian brown hawk, stared impassively back at its smaller cousin. Maddie hurried to open the window, allowing the two birds to stare eye to eye. Faint clicking and a fainter hum came from the pair. After a bit, the hawk looked away. TD hopped to the table. He peered up at Maddie and warbled. She bent close.

"Speak."

Instead of cheery chirps, a man's voice issued from the shiny beak. "Mad-kin, saw you at aerodrome today." Aha! Maddie's old shipmate, Oberon O'Reilly, possessor of TD's twin, Tweetle-C. Obie went on, "Heard you were in Venice lately, kicking up your heels. Seems odd if you're trying for a low profile but you must have had reason. Figured I'd missed you here, glad you're back. If it's safe to meet up somewhere for a pint and a natter, send word to TC."

Maddie leaned down. "Tweetle-D, listen. To Oberon O'Reilly via Tweetle-C. Obie, it wasn't me in Venice. Some woman is using my name. If Father hears, I'm doomed. Ask Madame to have her investigated if possible. I'm at Shepheard's Hotel, Cairo. Dress in best uniform and you can appear here unremarked any day. Ask for Miss Maddie Hatter. SO glad you are here; why are you here? Oh, and find out anything about Baron Bodmin and his airship, the *Jules Verne*, too. Ta."

TD communed with the hawk again, and then it leapt from the windowsill with a startlingly lifelike cry. As it soared away into the afternoon's heat-haze, Maddie sank onto a chair with a sense of relief quite unbecoming to a modern, independent young woman. After a moment she straightened and reached for the inkwell. There, in the hidden compartment, was a single remaining visiting card. Whew! She was not entirely stranded. Then she noticed the bent corner. It meant, "Called while you were out."

Chapter Five

"THE UNMITIGATED gall of that woman!" Maddie finished her recounting of yesterday's events rather louder than she'd begun.

Obie wafted the lieutenant's white hat he held in one hand, disturbing the dark curls on his forehead. "My, but you are hot under that delightful collar. Understandably so. If Madame is delayed, I will make inquiries when my ship next touches at Venice."

"Well, thanks for that. Maybe I won't be summoned home in a hand-basket just yet." Maddie cast her eyes up at the archway on the second-floor landing. In her chamber, TD was romping with his twin, under orders to hide on top of the armoire if anyone came in. Could he be tweaked to click images of any future intruders? "Nice uniform. Did you re-enlist in the Navy?"

Obie flashed very white teeth, under blue eyes

sparkling with mischief. "If you can be incognito, so can I. Besides, you said to wear my best uniform, and the crew's togs of the White Sky Line are nothing to shout about."

"You're working on White Sky liners? Have you ever seen the owner, Miss, or Mrs. White?"

"Mrs. Midas-White," he corrected. "Not personally, but I've flown with her aboard. And we've all heard the instructions: skimp everybody but the First Class passengers. Not that there's much room for other classes; a half-deck of business travelers and missionaries in Second, almost inside the envelope, and amidships are servants and crew, all stacked up like pants in a press. But oh, the First Class is luxury itself. Huge staterooms, velvet everywhere, real wood paneling and lead-crystal glassware. Old hat to you, but smart enough for us plebs. Actual books in the library, which, I might add, is half the width of the hull and almost as long as the main dining room. They hold entertainments there, visiting lecturers and opera singers, that sort of thing. Doesn't get my blood pumping like a dance-party on a surface ship, but what can you do?

"Anyway, the old lady's got claws for fingers. For real," he added as Maddie's eyebrows rose. "Metal claw-things, a couple on each hand, that she uses for counting her money and poking anybody who wastes supplies. I saw her draw blood on a drinks steward, and all for letting a few drops extra fall into a snifter."

"How many White Sky routes have you traveled?" Maddie listened with half an ear while she watched the nearest brass monkey. It would lower its paws from over its eyes to signal the daily aethernet news from London. Her article detailing the baron's lavish spending and his investor's identity might not have made the morning edition, but surely her earlier article about his friendships with Colonel Muster and Professor Plumb would appear today. She would still be "Our Correspondent in Cairo," but the words would be hers.

Their coffee arrived before the aethernet update. They sipped while Obie recounted what he'd learned of the *Jules Verne* from his privileged position as an aerodrome insider.

"The labourers are worried about the *Verne's* reverse-blower or its battery pack. Either might have failed over the desert. You know anything about the airship's condition?"

"Not until I find someone up in Cornwall to look it over. What's a reverse blower?"

"In desert travel, air-cooled engines can suck up a lot of dust over the course of a day. So, once a day or more, they disengage, and the fans turn in the opposite direction, drawing a mighty whoosh of filtered air out through them, carrying away any collected grit before it can damage the machinery. Battery-powered, since the engine has to be off while it happens. Then the engine starts up again, the right way around, and recharges the batteries for the next day's cleaning."

"And they think this might have failed on the baron's airship? But that wouldn't send him overboard, surely? No risk to him or the ship except that she was adrift. Why not wait for land and signal for help?"

"I understand his ship was almost over England anyway. No sandstorms to speak of at that latitude. None of us believe it got all the way there without him aboard, either. Mark my words, he'll be found in England or France."

France? Bodmin's nephew had been in France when the news of the disappearance got out. Was that a coincidence, or was he helping his uncle—very much alive—escape the investor's vengeance? After a moment she realized Obie was saying something about trans-oceanic crossings.

He repeated, "I said, I'm going to bid for America again as soon as we reach London, and then try for cross-country to California. Wouldn't you love to come along?"

"Not enough to work on a White Sky ship. A servant wouldn't be permitted to wander the First Class areas or attend the entertainments."

"True enough. Although it's a fair question whether even you, with all your book-learning, would find entertainment in a pair of professors arguing the location of a lost Nubian city when neither had ever set foot in a desert before. My pal Hiram was on duty up there, said half the audience nodded off."

"Lost Nubian city? Was one of them a Professor Plumb? Cambridge man, who favours smoking robes over dinner jackets?"

Obie shrugged. "Sounds like the English bloke, I guess. Beard like sheep's fleece, spoke like a prime minister. The other fellow was a Yankee through and through. Leather coat always, and a pistol under it. Simple name. Smith?" He shook his head.

"Jones?"

"Ah, that's the man. Professor Windsor Jones, Junior. From Indiana State University. Told me and Hiram about the wide open lands and skies. You can fly over the middle of America for three days without crossing a good-sized hill."

Obie took his leave before luncheon, saying he had that night's watch and wanted to sleep a bit first. "We're leaving day after tomorrow, as soon as the sands warm sufficiently to assist the lift. Leave early and pay for that pound of extra fuel? Not on the White Sky Line, I assure you." He kissed her cheek and strode away, tipping his hat in passing to Lady HH's nieces, who were eyeing him with frank appraisal.

Maddie hurried upstairs to let TC out of her window, and admired how his painted feathers blended effortlessly into the cityscape. Maybe she should ask Madame about getting TD a paint job. She fed the little bird his weekly power pellet and sat down to compose a brief article about Mrs. Midas-White and the possibility of a reverse-blower failure. Then she flipped back to her Christmas notebook to confirm her hunch: Jones was the man Professor Plumb feared would learn of his association with Baron Bodmin.

So the professors had traveled together from America. They and the baron shared an interest in things Nubian; did that include the legendary Eye of Africa? Perhaps Jones was entitled to a share if Bodmin found it. Which led back to the question: could Baron Bodmin have deliberately abandoned his airship, in order to be presumed dead, rather than share the proceeds with his investor or anyone else?

And where did Colonel Muster, the last of the baron's claimed expedition supporters, fit in? Muster was handling the baron's estate while he was away, and would doubtless have to disperse it when eventually the baron was pronounced dead. If a treasure had been found, the estate would become immensely more complicated as various interested parties tried to claim a share. Otherwise, it was simple: the whole lot went to the nephew. Maybe Muster, too, could claim a share if the mask was found?

Tweetle-D

Speculation was fruitless until another source of information turned up. Maddie closed the notebook and got down to writing a by-the-number article on hair adornments seen on ladies at breakfast, luncheon, tea, and supper during Spring in Cairo. For this, she could still get paid.

As she approached the dining room a scant hour

later, pink Clarice grasped her arm, gasping something so quietly that Maddie barely made out the word, "vanished."

"Speak up."

Clarice took a deep breath. "Colonel Muster is disgraced in London, vanished from his home, and feared dead by his own hand." As Maddie stared at her, she added, "So maybe he was lying about the widow and she really was a broken-hearted soldier's wife."

"She may have been a soldier's wife once for all I know, but I doubt very much if that was her real name."

"You investigated her?"

Maddie ignored that. "How did you hear about the colonel? He's been gone from Egypt more than three months."

"It's in the aether-news. The whole dining room is a-buzz."

"Go in to luncheon. I'll be there shortly." Maddie hurried toward the nearest brass monkey and fiddled a penny out of her pocketbook. She yanked over a chair and sat fidgeting while the monkey rolled forward, opening its vest. Then she scrolled, and scrolled, through screens of tiny letters and slightly larger headlines until CARDSHARP COLONEL caught her eye. She cranked up the magnifier to read the article.

The Floating Fortress,
England's Aeronautical Weekly

CARDSHARP COLONEL EJECTED
FROM ST. JAMES CLUB

According to reliable witnesses, Colonel Bilious Muster, long an habitué of fashionable gaming clubs on St. James Street, London, was recently ejected from the Royal Air Arms. The club refused to confirm or deny the incident, citing member privacy, but rumours fly of Muster's cheating at piquet and failure to pay his club dues. Creditors are encamped outside the retired officer's lodging, where the landlady admitted his rent is also in arrears.

The Colonel's downfall is all the more shocking as his service record is filled with battle honours. His earliest post was with the high-altitude scouts, who spend many hours aloft in tethered balloons to report enemy troop movements. These daring aeronauts were constantly at risk from enemy snipers and vagaries of weather, with only a canvas canopy to slow their descent should their balloon be ruptured. Muster earned three valorous medals aloft before returning to the Airship Services' Marine Corps for many further years of honourable service.

Muster's absence from his usual haunts went unremarked for some days, until this reporter sought him out for reaction to the disappearance of his friend, Baron Bodmin. Fellow club-men disagree whether he was ejected before or after Bodmin's airship was found adrift. Some hope he is living modestly on substantial winnings from Sir Ambrose Peacock, while others suggest he followed a long tradition for disgraced military men, i.e. an honourable suicide by service revolver.

It was true then. Colonel Muster was discredited, and nowhere was Maddie credited, even indirectly, for sending reporters to find him. If he was dead, and the baron was in or near England—either dead or alive—then the story's Egyptian roots were dead too, at least as far as earning Maddie a byline.

Now what?

There was still the mysterious widow who had usurped Maddie's identity and possibly many others. Fifty years on from the publication of that novel about conniving Becky Sharp, English readers remained fascinated by beautiful schemers. But no story could be attempted until Madame sent word of investigative results in Venice. What if she could not justify using her family's spies for Maddie's very minor (to a worldwide corporation) problem?

With drooping ruffles, Maddie went into luncheon, prepared on principle to keep her ears open about the colonel, the baron, and the widow, while her eyes recorded the cuffs, collars, ascots, and waistcoats worn by those illustrious guests who had not yet fled the heat of Egypt for the moderate climes of Italy or France.

Chapter Six

THE CHATTER AT luncheon interspersed people's previously suppressed suspicions about the colonel with which liner each party had booked on for the return to Europe. As Lady HH put it in her brook-no-argument way, "No lady of breeding wishes to be caught in Cairo when the heat makes public perspiration unavoidable."

Maddie was struck by the realization that her source of fashion columns was fleeing the desert and taking her income with it. Would CJ reassign her or consider their association at an end? Or worse: expect her to eke out an existence in Cairo until next winter's call for foreign fashions. Waiting around had never been her strongest suit. She would ask outright for a reassignment to a European city, and she knew just which one. As luncheon and gossip wound down and the residents dispersed for postprandial naps or brandies, she dropped her napkin onto her plate and stood.

Clarice rose too. "Miss Hatter, may I accompany you upstairs? I feel quite in need of a rest today." They'd barely left the dining room before the girl brought up Sir Ambrose Peacock. "Is he still coming? Have you heard anything? We are booked to leave in two days! If I were to miss him here! I shall feign illness if I must, to delay our departure."

"I've heard nothing of his impending arrival," Maddie said. "All the aeronauts I've interviewed say his uncle is most likely to be found in England or France. He may well have seen fit to remain in that region."

The girl drooped. "Thank you," she said, and listlessly wandered off toward the ascender.

Maddie went straight to the message desk and printed out a fast telegraph form for CJ: *Rqst immdt reassg 2 Vnc Itly.* She handed it over and asked with some trepidation about incoming messages. There were none. The heavy hand of paternal ire had not fallen today, and would not, she hoped, until she could show Father evidence of the imposter and possibly a way to track the woman down.

She collected a British newspaper from a newly-printed stack on her way upstairs, on the scant chance that she had been credited for something, somewhere, on the many pages she had skimmed past at the brass monkey's vest. Twenty minutes later, she crumpled the newspaper with both hands, threw it to the carpet, and stamped on it. TD's little head tilted sideways to peer down at the sheet. The frowning face of a middle-aged woman glared up. Maddie stamped on it once more, but the screaming headline could not be eclipsed:

AMERICAN HEIRESS BADGERED
FOR BATTY BARON'S BILLS

Following the discovery of Baron Bodmin's abandoned airship, the Jules Verne, *his American investor is being urgently billed by London merchants who supplied the missing adventurer's expedition. The total owed is estimated in the thousands of guineas. On being informed the baron had not paid his bills before departing England, the lady used a word unprintable and fled the reporters.*

The only surviving child of the sole owner of the White Sky Line of trans-oceanic airships, Mrs. Midas-White is presently residing at Claridge's Hotel, London. Merchants' bailiffs are encamped on the street outside, with more arriving hourly. Foreign creditors are expected to join the throng. Merchants in Cairo claim the Midas-White name was pledged in Egypt for luxurious lodgings and lavish parties as well as outfitting the Jules Verne *for desert travel.*

How much the heiress had already advanced in support of Bodmin's latest dream is unknown. A few inquiries would have shown the venturesome baron's previous investors were long since soured by his unfruitful quests for legendary treasures.

"They only found Mrs. Midas-White because I told them who to seek," Maddie seethed. "Merchants in Cairo indeed. I could be a brass monkey for all the advancement my investigations have wrought." She stomped across the room and back, and jabbed a finger toward the crushed paper on the carpet. "It serves them right if she refuses to speak to any male reporters. For all her tight-gloved reputation, I bet the baron charmed her into parting with money, and she is crushed by this evidence of his betrayal. She might tell a sympathetic woman reporter a sad and cautionary tale. Oh, if I were in London today! I could get that interview."

She was not in London, nor likely to be. CJ might approve her relocation to Venice but working in London, where the risk of being recognized as Lord Main-Bearing's missing daughter was exceedingly high, was never in her future. No, she was in Cairo another few days at least, and had stories to file.

She spent the afternoon composing a week's worth of articles centered on Lady HH's new Easter bonnet. This immense edifice of wire, linen, and lilies was worthy of a cathedral, and would be seen in one on Easter Sunday in London. Maddie had been granted an early viewing as a means of advertising where the nieces might be soonest seen. The London Season kicked off at Easter, and advance publicity for suitable girls might lead to early offers of marriage.

Poor Clarice. Her heart was spoken for, but her hand would go to the party deemed most satisfactory to her family. Perhaps Maddie would be invited to cover the wedding. She could wear a hat with a veil, dress in half-mourning as a disguise, and pass unremarked beneath the very noses of her parents' friends. It would only be a violation of Father's decree if she were recognized.

The next morning brought one message, not from Father, for which she was grateful, but from CJ.

"No."

Maddie crushed the flimsy paper in her fist, heedless of the purple ink smearing her last pair of spotless net gloves. She looked for the nearest ashtray, intent on condemning the missive as well as CJ to perdition by the fastest route. Before she could ask the elderly major seated there for a match, he started up out of his chair and hurried away talking to himself.

"My word, my word. I say, wot! That baron feller is dead after all. Must tell Neddy." Maddie slid into a chair uncomfortably warm from his rotund rear and found the news on his open brass monkey:

The Cornwall Cog and Goggles

BODMIN'S BODY FOUND— MYSTERY DEEPENS

The mortal remains of Baron Bodmin have washed ashore in Cornwall, only a few miles from isolated Bodmin Manor. The remains, much diminished by the action of waves and sea creatures, were lashed to a small, but weighty, White Sky Line trunk.

Those who discovered the body immediately opened the trunk, hoping to be the first to see the fabled Nubian treasure the baron sought in Africa, but were disappointed to find only books and papers, some of them damaged by water seepage.

Coast Guard officials say the trunk could not have floated and was probably dragged inshore by the tide over a number of days. The cork belt and escape canopy missing from the adrift airship were not located with the body, and it is unknown whether he had lost or traded them earlier on his expedition rather than using them to escape from what he must have deemed a foundering airship.

Why Bodmin should have elected to abandon ship with a heavy trunk is unknown. Local sea-goers say he might have bailed out at low altitude over shallow water and hoped to drag the trunk ashore safely. Whether the tide set against him or the wind was offshore cannot be known unless the time of his entering the sea can be determined by other means.

As Obie had predicted, Baron Bodmin was dead, and in England. There was no story at all left in Cairo, and the sooner Maddie left the better. She returned to the hotel's long marble reception counter and told the clerk, "Have my steamer trunk sent to my chamber."

Chapter Seven

IT WAS NOT easy to get passage out of Cairo at the pinnacle of the English departures. First the hotel's travel concierge declined to book her a stateroom, saying sternly that most guests had booked weeks ago. Then, after delay while he pretended to adjust the magnification of his brass monoculus, he eventually wrote out the address of the nearest respectable airship booking office.

It was quite a walk on a hot morning, through streets alive with beggars, hawkers, business people striding along, and women, unseen under veils or enveloping chadors, gliding with baskets on their heads or loads on their backs. Horse-drawn carriages competed with piled-high donkeys and self-propelling drays, while occasional camels sneered at them all. Everywhere children darted, calling for baksheesh and occasionally picking the pockets of distracted shoppers.

The clerk at the booking office was firm: the only available space this week was a First Class parlour-stateroom (with balcony) on a White Sky liner leaving for Venice tomorrow morning. The money was available from unspent quarterly allowances, but it would cost Maddie more than she had earned during her entire Cairo stay. She shook her head.

"What about the following week?"

By then, the clerk informed her, the spaces were mostly booked for archaeological staff. Except, of course, for a First Class parlour stateroom . . .

Maddie walked out, convinced the clerk was getting a fat commission on First Class parlour-staterooms (with balconies). How was she to get back to Europe without beggaring herself?

A hawk's cry overhead gave her a possible answer. She hurried back to Shepheard's Hotel, ignored a wave from Clarice as she crossed the vast lobby, and took the stairs to her room. As the safragi came along, tapping at doors to warn of the imminence of luncheon, she summoned TD down from his perch on the armoire.

"TD, listen to me. To Oberon O'Reilly via Tweetle-C. Obie, I've got to get out of Cairo. Can you get me a job on your airship by tomorrow? I don't care what." Heedless for once of anyone seeing—after all, she would be gone soon, one way or another—she sent the little bird out the window, up to the rooftop in a flash of brass wings, to await the first messenger-hawk that passed. She tidied her hair, tucked her pink sequined notebook into her handbag, and went down to lunch.

When she came upstairs, with a few brief notes on end-of-season fashions that might make just one more Foreign Fashionista column, her steamer trunk stood in the middle of the room. She occupied the rest of the afternoon sorting her clothing, discarding those too light for spring in Europe and reluctantly parting with two of her five hats. The first chambermaid who came along would doubtless snatch her leavings but that was no matter when Maddie was determined to be in Venice within a week to start tracking down her imposter. With that chore out of the way, she sat in one of the hard, straight chairs and watched the sun-baked strip of blue sky above. TD had returned, his message transferred, but there was yet no sign of a hawk carrying a return message from Obie.

The sky darkened. Those pedestrians below who had not already gone home for a nap fled to the nearest arched arcades. Maddie stuck her head out the window and looked up, just in time for a whirling dust devil to pepper her with upswept grit. She sputtered and pulled back as the first fat raindrops pelted down. The window banged on its hinges. A wet gust billowed the curtain and the bed's mosquito netting. She grabbed the window and forced it closed. No hawks would fly in this. How could she go calmly down to dinner with her whole future in the air somewhere between the hotel and the aerodrome?

She climbed into her only unpacked dinner dress, a simply-cut, pale green silk with matching cording around the neck and in two widening lines down her front. It was one she had worn as a debutante, thus two years out of date and readily identifiable as such by the miniscule puff in the cap sleeves. Downstairs she went, slowly, seeing for perhaps the last time the lobby lit for evening, with its gas wall sconces flaring and its brass floor lamps giving off their steady, steam-generated, electrical glow. The lights picked out every message-disc that crawled along the walls, and shone upon the monocles and oculii of the gentlemen as much as on the ladies' jewels. Up in the highest windows, those barely more than vents for the day's heat, small glimmers showed the window-automatons, already crawling along with their brushes scrubbing away any dust and streaks left by the storm. She hoped none had been hit by lightning; the ones that came off her father's manor in storms died sparking and writhing, their bright metal blackened and warped by the powerful currents.

Contemplating the deaths of automatons, she didn't notice Clarice and the blue niece—Nancy—waiting at the bottom of the stairs. They stepped forward as she reached the lobby floor.

"Miss Hatter?"

Her first impulse was to brush them and their silly, girlish preoccupations away, but the worry in their faces stopped her. "What is the matter?"

Chapter Eight

MADDIE LEFT CAIRO in the morning, not in a servants' stacked and airless berth, but in the full comfort of a First Class parlour-stateroom (with balcony) for which she had not paid one slim farthing, and where Obie himself might at some point be required to serve her tea as part of his normal duties. All those column inches devoted to Lady HH's hats and nieces over the winter had produced this miracle. On the very eve of that lady's scheduled departure, she had come down with an illness too intestinally disturbing to allow her to travel, and she urgently required a genteel female companion to escort her nieces as far as Venice.

"In Venice," had said Clarice earnestly, so worried that her usual pinkness was the merest shimmer on her fair cheeks, "our cousin will be waiting for us, straight from England, with her seamstress and the fabrics for our presentation gowns. We're to be fitted and the gowns made during the journey, for our presentation at Court is the very first Drawing Room after Easter."

"So you see," Nancy added, "we really must leave Cairo on the morrow, or we shall miss our only meeting with the Royal Princesses. A snub of that magnitude would disgrace us forever."

Clarice was watching Maddie with the concentration of a hawk after a pigeon, and misinterpreted the terror that washed over her at the thought of being trapped afloat with exactly the type of people she had promised her father to avoid.

"You needn't fear you will be stuck with us if Lucy is delayed; she married a Steamlord's son, and *they*, you know, are never afflicted with delays because they travel in their own air yachts."

"Hers is quite large enough for several more people," Nancy offered, "if you would like to come with us all the way to England."

As the nieces alternated in cajoling and explaining, Maddie caught her breath and faced her terror squarely. She had passed the winter unremarked amidst that very class of English traveler, and many of the people here now would be fellow passengers. They would assuredly not look further than the ink-daubed fingers and sequined notebook of the lady journalist. The only risk was the moment of meeting the Steamlord's new daughter-in-law, and she might be a complete unknown.

"I'll consider it," she said, cutting off the girls in mid-flow. "Take me to your aunt."

They had, and, all arrangements being satisfactory, here she was, floating above the Nile in a blue velvet chair with gold cording, her gaze alternating between the view and a cunning Sphinx-shaped fountain that burbled in the corner. An iced-coffee service stood at her elbow. She stretched, delighted at the temporary return to that world from which she had exiled herself. The nieces shared a smaller bedchamber that opened off her parlour, under her eye and underfoot for the entire passage. Their maid, a dour person of uncertain age, was doubtless accommodated in one of the airless, viewless, cramped berths that might have been Maddie's lot had the hawk with Obie's message not been delayed by yesterday's storm.

The only point of risk was the handover in Venice, but that should prove no real problem. Cousin Lucy had married into an Artificer family, a full generation newer and one rung lower than the Main-Bearings. Father would not be intimate with any family that carried a taint of Spanish in its bloodline, as the Aquatiempe did. In any case, the marriage of the third son had occurred after Maddie's unorthodox exit from London Society, and Lucy herself was an Old Nobility baronet's daughter three years younger. Their paths would never have crossed.

The trip up the Nile was innocuous. The girls were content to sit upon the shady balcony much of the day, eyeing the archaeological ruins that passed beneath the airship's keel and gossiping about their fellow passengers. None of these were young men either handsome or eligible, and Maddie's first fear, that she would be forced to chaperone the girls everywhere to ward off undesirable attention, had fallen away with the last sight of the Great Pyramid at Giza.

After luncheon, they explored the facilities.

Clarice and Nancy were no strangers to airship liners, but Maddie, until she had run away, had traveled like any Steamlord child, in private luxury. To her, the fittings of the various regions were not especially luxurious, but after two years of living as a working woman, she relished the comfort of servants to bring a cool drink, the latest newspapers, and blank aetherogram forms on request.

After a whirlwind pass through the dining room, First-Class Lounge, Spa facilities (with a rather ominous masseuse offering her services in or out of the steam-closets) and an outdoor viewing platform complete with chaises from which one could comfortably view the passing scenery, Maddie settled in the ship's library. She looked around at the heavy books on the inner wall, the flimsier airship editions of popular works on the other walls, and the large globe of the Known World, with its uncharted spaces over the poles left blank. This might be the very room in which the two professors had argued over Nubian cities and, possibly, treasures. That was unlikely, given the vast number of White Sky Line airships circling the world, but surely the room itself was similar in most aspects.

Thinking about the unsolved mystery of the baron's death only reminded her of her failure to find the widow. Where in Venice could she begin her search for the imposter? She had only visited once before, as Madame Taxus-Hemlock's lab assistant, and barely long enough to attend a rather riotous embassy party most memorable for Obie's dramatic departure. He had leapt across a canal to the opposite balcony by moonlight, scaled the wall to the rooftop, and flown away on a small private runabout that had carelessly left a rope ladder dangling as it lifted off. Maddie did not fear being recognized at the embassy, if chance took her there. Back then, she had been wearing purple goggles that matched her hair, and a laboratory smock much stained with exotic hues and some odd scents as well. Miss Maddie Hatter, journalist, had never been to Venice before.

That evening, with the girls safely in their stateroom preparing for bed, Maddie took a turn on the stern viewing platform. It was deserted, for few passengers braved the sharp, clean tang of the desert by night. She had seen Obie going about his duties several times that day, and knew he would look for her when he could. Meanwhile, she could look out over the desert below, its rocky outcrops and sloping dunes tinted blue by a waxing moon that shimmered over crests and limned each sandy windrow in purple shadow. Concerns of the civilized world were as ants beneath the weight of mere survival down there; up here, too, her worries faded before the vast empty majesty of the land and sky, the whisper of the night-time breeze teasing the sand into new patterns for the next morning. A bird warbled, alone in the immensity.

It warbled again, very close. She turned her head as TC landed on her shoulder, his little brass claws folding lightly into the fabric of her gown.

"Hello, little bird," she said, and touched its head by way of greeting. "Where's your master?"

"Just coming," said a voice from above, and a dark shape swung down from the crew catwalk suspended below the great liner's envelope. Obie landed almost as lightly as his bird and joined her at the rail. "Lovely night."

"It is that." Maddie sighed. "Looking at this endless sand, my worries seem so small. I ran out on my job in Cairo and might lose my allowance or my freedom over that woman's antics in Venice. I have no idea how to go about finding and exposing her, or if I should even try, when to call attention to her will reveal to Society that I am choosing to live away from my family. But at least I am not struggling to survive the desert."

Obie patted her hand. "Madame Taxus-Hemlock will have that imposter sorted by the time we arrive in Venice."

"You seem very certain of that. What if she can't waste her family's minions on my little problem?"

"Of course she will. You're her protégé. Reminding her of her younger self and all that. Anyway, she'll send a message to the ship when we're in range. You'll see. And then you can decide what to do. This ship is only hanging about in Venice overnight, but I'll have shore leave and can help you get started."

"Thanks, Obie. You're a great pal in a tight spot."

He said nothing by reply, and they leaned on the rail in companionable silence. After a while, he asked, "Were you still curious about those two professors?"

"Sort of. Why?"

"My mate, Hiram, was the steward on their corridor during that Atlantic crossing. He'll tell you all about them if you like."

"I'd like that. When and where?"

"Let's aim for tomorrow evening, same time?"

"Same place, too?"

"Nope. This platform will be crowded tomorrow

night. The ship has a shore day in Athens, departing at sunset, but hovers near those famous ruins if the moon is full enough for a view."

"The Parthenon by moonlight? I will have to bring the girls out for that. After they're in bed, where can we meet that won't be conspicuous?"

"I'll bring Hiram along to you," said Obie. "Anyone who sees two crew members going into your stateroom will merely think you are irate about something. First Class gets the kid glove treatment, remember?"

The next day was a repeat of the first, save that they woke over the Mediterranean off the fabled Greek Isles. Morning passed quietly as they enjoyed the crisp sea breeze on their private balcony, watching while passengers and luggage were winched to the roof of the Athens terminal. Those passengers staying with the ship were offered an afternoon's excursion to the National Archaeological Museum, but the girls declared they had seen quite enough archaeology in Egypt and were content to stay on board, playing deck sports with other young people. Maddie took herself off to the Library and the new day's aethernet news. It wasn't long before a familiar name caught her eye: Professor Windsor Jones, Junior.

The University Times

AMERICAN LECTURER
LAUGHED OUT OF OXFORD

Professor Windsor "Windy" Jones, a scholar visiting from a middle-American "university," gave a detailed description of a fabled proto-Nubian mask, The Eye of Africa, at the Explorers Club dinner in Balliol College last week. He embellished the telling with convincing detail.

When asked to produce evidence of his conclusions, Jones claimed his research was all lost on his airship voyage to England last fall. The White Sky Line denies any claim was made by Mr. Jones for lost luggage. His research cast into grave doubt, Jones' visiting-professor status at Oxford has been terminated. The rest of his British lecture tour dates are in doubt.

An American, Professor Jones did not depart with the dignity of a British don. After confronting an esteemed Cambridge professor in the dining hall with accusations of theft, Jones was escorted from the Sacred Halls of Academe. At the university gate he yelled, "I'm right and I'll rub all your noses in it."

The egregious insult has cast further doubt on the recent contentious policy of treating America's fledgling academic institutes as on par with the venerable universities of England. Look for sparks to fly at next month's meeting of the Oxford-Cambridge Guild.

Maddie raised her eyes from the brass monkey's vest to the wide sky outside. Professor Jones was an expert on the Eye of Africa mask, and claimed his research had been stolen on his trans-oceanic passage. Could Professor Plumb have absconded with Jones' research, and provided it to Baron Bodmin? Did either of the academic gentlemen have cause to engineer the death of the baron? Once the matter of the imposter was settled, Maddie would make her way closer to England and poke her nose more deeply into both professors' movements. There was more to this Bodmin death to be explored, and the byline might be within her grasp after all.

That night, after an hour spent gazing upon the ancient wonder that was the ruined Parthenon, its crumbled columns and tumbled stones ghostly white in the clear moonlight, she shepherded the girls into their beds.

"Tomorrow we will come to Venice, after which you will be very busy getting ready for your Court presentations. Tonight, you must rest. I will speak to the crew this evening, to ensure you and your luggage are transferred directly to your cousin's air-yacht with all possible dispatch." That last would cover the situation if either girl woke later and heard male voices in the parlour.

As the hour grew late, she began to fear some wakeful matron would spot two male crew members slipping at midnight into the stateroom of a young, attractive female passenger. That would ruin the reputation of this identity completely, and she would have to start afresh in some other arena. She was about to give up and prepare for bed herself when a bird warbled from the balcony. TD, bored with his day's confinement to the wardrobe, answered it. There, at the balcony doorway, stood Obie, his hand raised to tap.

"What on earth are you doing out there?" Even as she asked, she knew the answer. Obie, as a midshipman on that experimental Navy craft where they'd first met, had often taken unconventional routes around the outside of the airship. He had no fear of the altitude, and rather too great a belief in his own ability to move about the envelope's netting in perfect safety. Behind him stood another young man in crew whites, looking rather like a long-legged crane and quite sanguine about his external scramble along the great ship's envelope. Clearly this fellow was a kindred spirit to the adventurous Obie.

Obie introduced his shipmate. "Miss Maddie Hatter, meet Hiram Phillips, great-grandson of the captain of the first settlement ship to reach Australia. He can tell you all about those professors." Hiram Phillips bowed slightly, a courtesy due to any First Class passenger, even Maddie Hatter, lady reporter, whose status on solid ground was barely higher than that of an airship steward. She tipped her head to him, whipped out her pink sequined notebook, and invited both men to sit.

"Mr. Phillips, please tell me: what do you remember of professors Windsor Jones and Polonius Plumb on their crossing last fall? Did they spend a lot of time together? Did they argue much? Do you remember anything they discussed? Did Professor Jones misplace any research materials?"

Hiram stared at her. "Now how did you know about that, Miss? The crew made no report."

"So his research did go missing?"

"Yeah, s'right. Last night o' the crossing it was, sky calm as a millpond. The professors were elbow-bending a-plenty. Professor Jones has to be drunk to fly at all, but this was a big 'un. Started in the bar and went on to Jones' stateroom in Second Class. They were in there for hours, yarning and looking at papers and charts, ringing for more brandy. Last time I went by, maybe four in the morning, door was open and Mr. Jones was snoring with his head on a bare desk. I shoved him onto his berth, stripped off his boots, and shut his door on the way out.

"Next morning, they thought he was gone ashore with the rest but cleaners found him still abed. He woke up ranting about his trunk of papers being gone. Day crew had no idea what he meant, just hurried him ashore with promises it had been offloaded with the rest of the luggage. We went straight on to Paris and never heard another word from him."

"Ah. And did Professor Plumb disembark in London too?"

"That he did. When Obie said you was interested, I asked around. Plumb were one o' the first off the ship. Nobody remembers how much luggage he had. Not after a whole winter's weekly crossings."

"Thank you, Hiram." Maddie smiled, and then, at a faint sound from the small stateroom's door, asked how to get her charges transferred to a private airship the following afternoon. Obie said finding a Steamlord yacht at the terminal would be peaches and cream.

"Just you ready them and their luggage when you see Venice off the port bow, likely around teatime, and I'll pop by with porters as soon as we hook onto the terminal. Bring you any news at the same time."

"Thank you, Obie." After checking for long-nosed matrons, she saw the two young men out into the corridor and went to bed, worrying how to proceed in Venice if no message came from Madame to help direct her actions.

On the third morning since Cairo, the airship cruised low along the Dalmatian coast, over unfolding views of rocky crags, green fields, and stony medieval towns with orange tiled roofs. It was not yet teatime when Venice rose out of the sea in the distance, its islands verdant and its buildings antique cream in the misty sunlight.

Obie arrived with the porters, and said in quick, quiet tones, "The imposter's long gone. On arrival in February, she stayed a week at the Lido Hotel under your name, vanished for a month, and then departed on a White Sky liner as you again."

A small mercy: she had not spent all of Carnivale carousing as a Main-Bearing. "Going where?"

"Paris-London, same as us. Only thing is, she never got off in either place. Not under any name Madame's minions could discover."

"She switched names on me again? How will I ever find her now?" And what was to stop the woman switching back to Maddie's name whenever convenient?

"Madame says if you will come straight up to London, she may have more answers by the time you arrive there."

"London! Oh, Obie, that's a terrific risk."

"What else can you do? Where else would you go?"

Clarice, in the parlour doorway, exclaimed. "You're going? Oh, please, not yet, Miss Hatter. You must turn us over to Lucy in person."

"Yes, of course I will take you to your cousin," Maddie assured her. She'd long ago worked out that Lucy was no threat to her identity. An Aquatiempe, possibly a sister of the groom, had attended pre-Season dance classes at the same academy as Maddie in the same year, but she would be far away in London. No Steamlord's daughter would interrupt her all-important dress-fittings to supervise the return of two little cousins by marriage. "I was merely asking whether there would be an affordable stateroom to London, for this one is too large for me alone."

"You're going on to London at once?" Clarice clapped her hands. "Come with us. The yacht has bags of staterooms. And surely you could write a column about our Court dresses?" Maddie's eyes met Obie's. He shrugged. She did too. As a way to get to London, it had the merits of being both fast and free.

"Yes, I will come, if your cousin permits." She swept up her wide hat, with TD already nestled amongst the metallic ribbons, and pinned it into place.

In a very short time, Maddie, Clarice, and Nancy were walking down the gangplank to the Venetian aerodrome. The greeny-gray waters of the Grand Canal murmured four floors below, but the gangplank was wide and the side-rails sturdy oak. Their trunks, bags, and hatboxes followed in a veritable parade of porters. Mist kissed their cheeks, too delicate to be called rain, but leaving a slick over the vast, flat rooftop with its contra-dance of passengers, porters, and luggage.

At the last step, a man in majordomo's livery of black and teal—the Aquatiempe colours, Maddie recognized—lay in wait for them. A phalanx of one-wheeled automatons stood behind him, their armatures ready to take the load from the porters. Steamer trunks would be towed while smaller boxes were piled on their polished platforms. The ladies, the majordomo indicated with a bow and an outstretched hand, would be conveyed across the terminal in a teacup-shaped, auto-steering steam-carriage, painted and upholstered in teal with black accents. Trust an Artificer family to have the best and newest automatons.

The mist thickened to dampening droplets. An umbrella rose from the teacup's rim and spread itself over the cushioned area. Its surface shifted hues with each raindrop, making an ever-changing mosaic of water-scapes from deep blue to palest green around a core palette of purest teal. The pole slid upward to permit easy entry to the semicircular seat, and then lowered itself to a distance safe for hat trimmings, its angles optimized for deflecting rain from passengers. As soon as the ladies were seated, the teacup turned on its saucer and rolled smoothly away, its steam-driven wheels making less sound than the clockwork mechanism that guided it.

Hearing the tiny chuff of released steam above the ticking, Maddie knew a small thrill of family pride. Her great-grandfather had introduced the first bronze bearing that allowed a step-down in power from a steam-driven mechanism to a clockwork one, opening up the world to wondrous steam-and-clockwork constructions, including self-propelling, self-guiding vehicles like this one. For that invention a grateful Empire had created him the third-ever Steamlord, and awarded him the family heraldic alloy of bronze. To that one invention the family ever since owed its prosperity. Not so thrilling was the old man's use of an entirely unrelated technology to tinker with the family's genetic heritage and turn all their hair bronze with a single black streak. Dying over that gleaming metallic hue, on lashes and brows as well as scalp, was one of

Maddie's more irksome grooming tasks. But nothing the Aquatiempe had accomplished would have been possible without her great-grandfather's bronze, step-down, power bearing.

Across the terminus they went, the teacup gliding this way and that through the clusters of passengers and multi-cart baggage trains. Obie walked beside it, the majordomo behind, his automatons following him with the trunks and hat-boxes. Above the buzz of wheels, voices, and airship engines, Obie pointed out to the nieces the airships of various nations' fleets, the Greek Royal Barge, and the Venetian Doge's personal craft, which was rumoured to be used largely to ferry visiting Vatican officials to discreet gaming establishments.

"Hah," said Maddie. "Nothing in Venice is discreet. Some pleasures are merely more expensive than others for the quality of their illusion of discretion." Too late she realized the discussion might be straying into waters unsuitable for sheltered English debutantes, but the girls were not attending. Instead, they looked ahead eagerly for their first glimpse of their cousin's new family's air yacht. The procession halted beside an elaborately painted airship of considerable size. Its Carnivale mask motif was predominantly teal and black, ornamented with silver scrollwork and fist-sized crystals polished to the sheen of diamonds. This was what Maddie's father would consider vulgar ostentation. She stepped out of the saucer with the aid of Obie's hand and the teacup carried on, up a black gangplank railed by silver ropes.

Clarice called back, "Please hurry, Miss Hatter. Anyone will guide you to the ladies' parlour."

"Just thanking the nice officer," Maddie said. As the automatons flowed around them with the luggage, she asked Obie softly, "How can I find Madame in London?"

"I don't know if she's there yet," Obie replied. "She was en route from the Hungarian-Imperial Parasol Championships in Frankfurt. We haven't had a chance to get a message off save that we'd reached Venice and would advise, and we don't know how long that news will take to find her. What do you want me to pass on, since you can't send TD up from this garish vessel unseen?"

"Tell her . . . say I will go to Claridge's Hotel to seek an interview with Mrs. Midas-White, to save my job with CJ. Once I find a quiet professional ladies' club for the night, I'll let her know where to find me." Obie was about to protest, but Maddie shushed him. Yes, walking into Claridge's might put her into the path of ladies who had known her. However, she had often stayed there as Madame's assistant, in purple hair, a lab coat, and thick magnifying goggles, and would readily find another disguise to shield her from passing glances. She squeezed his hand, thanked him for his help, and followed the last automaton over the black gangplank.

Stepping inside was like going home. A human footman bowed and led her inward without daring to inquire of her identity or destination. The aerodrome noises hushed. The thick carpet gave beneath her boots. The servants stowing luggage stepped aside and lowered their gaze as she passed. It mattered not that the livery and carpets were not in her family's colours, or that the veneered walls with their raised scrollwork were black rather than brushed oak, or that the handrails, sconces, and doorknobs were silver instead of gleaming bronze. The whisper of steam in unseen pipes was the life-beat she had heard since the day of her birth. She relaxed and walked calmly onward, ready to face the young mistress of this magnificence.

At the bottom of a wide staircase, an oval foyer opened. Beyond an archway was the grand salon, consuming the forward quarter of the ship with its velvet, fringes, and panoramic view. To the left an open double door revealed a billiard table and other accoutrements of idle entertainment. The footman took her to the right, to an elegant parlour done in shades of teal from the silk damask upholstery and draperies to the flocked wallpaper. Even the ladies' gowns were teal, one conservatively cut as befit a young, brown-haired bride from the Old Nobility— Lucy—and the other a daring splash of turquoise tulle over a black lace dress slit so high up the thigh and down at the cleavage as to be barely there at all. Knee-high black boots and fingerless, black lace gloves completed the ensemble. One of the sisters-in-law had come along after all. Maddie quickly decided this must be a married woman, for no Steamlord papa would permit his unwed daughter out in such apparel.

The owner of the dashing couture looked at Maddie from under natural teal hair cut into numerous black-edged wedges. Her eyelashes were impossibly long, tipped with black hearts, over eyes painted in sweeps of water hues that mimicked the sea beyond the lagoon. The flawless artistry of the cheeks ended in deep teal lips shaped in the most perfectly plump cupid's bow Maddie had ever seen.

Surely the loveliest lips in London.

The lips . . . oh, hell. Serephene Aquatiempe, the one member of this family who might possibly have seen enough of the Honourable Madeleine to recognize her in Maddie's working-class face. And how under the heavens did she get away with that daring dress?

The room was bathed in the glaring electrical light most likely to highlight the greeny-bronze undertones beneath Maddie's mousy brown dye job. Exposure might occur as soon as she removed her hat. She cast her eyes down, tilting her wide blue brim forward to shield most of her face, and curtseyed clumsily, as if she had not been trained to it since birth. How could she spend the next thirty-six hours in close confines with this young lady and not be revealed? Better to claim air-sickness and keep to her stateroom. She repeated the curtsey to Lucy.

"I hope," she said, aping a Yorkshire accent as far as she dared, "the misses have not importuned you for me to join your family party. If this is not convenient, I will debark at once and find a place on a commercial airship."

"Bosh," said Serephene, her exquisite eyes fixed on Maddie still. "Lucy, dear, do take your cousins to their stateroom, and I will show the chaperone to her quarters. Come this way, Miss . . . Hatter."

Maddie followed. Nobody actually from the lesser orders refused a . . . request . . . from a Steamlord's daughter.

Serephene led the way along the starboard corridor, her tulle side-bustle briskly brushing the wall and a maid who was squeezed flat in a doorway to stay out of the lady's way. More black paneling and silver fittings, room upon room, broken by a single open space with wide windows, comfortable chairs, and bookshelves on either end. One lace-gloved hand waved in that direction.

"The library, such as it is. You will be right next to it, should you desire to read. Your choices are popular literature and dozens of treatises on the water-clock miniaturizations for which the English Crown found my grandfather worthy of a peerage. There's a brass monkey comes down from the ceiling; just hit the blue button on any chair-arm. We depart at once, and dine over the Alps. *En famille*, so you need not unpack an evening dress." She opened a door and ushered Maddie into a stateroom almost as comfortable as the one she'd had on her own father's air yacht. "Unless you'd like to borrow one of mine?"

"That would not be suitable, milady," said Maddie, "for one of my class."

"Pity," said Serephene. She opened a panel to show a bathing closet with full-sized tub and a wall filled with colourful jars, towels, sponges, scents, and at least eight shades of toenail lacquer. "I'd hoped you would admit it, and not force me to say so. I know who you are."

"I don't know what you're talking about, milady."

"Bosh, darling." The lady flung herself into an armchair tapestried with gondolas on water. "What I want to know is how you managed it. If I have to sleepwalk through one more Season shoving away the chinless would-be bridegrooms with the toe of my boot, I shall go utterly mad with boredom. You ran off two years ago, or were kidnapped, but anyway you have survived in a world in which we pampered daughters are expected to perish from sheer terror, and yet here you are, in blooming health. Although more shabbily dressed than I ever expected to see the Honourable Madeleine M—"

"Hush! All right then. It's me. And I was desperately hoping not to be recognized. If my father finds out I've come to London, I'll be forced home. Or worse."

"What could possibly be worse?"

"A convent in the Shetland Islands."

The magnificent eyes opened wide. "Your secret is safe. Tell me how you escaped."

Maddie sighed and sank into another armchair, spreading her two-year old skirt and wishing she dared appear, just once more, in a properly fitted gown of some decadent fabric.

"All right, but it's not something I recommend. I stole clothing and a satchel from my maid, covered the bronze in my hair with brown shoe-polish, and stowed away on a runabout that was moored near the Admiralty. They thought I was a servant, one who was late for duty. I ended up working for a strange lady botanist as her lab assistant, on a trip halfway around the world. When that one ended, she helped me negotiate a peace with my father and I got a job as a Fashionista. But only on condition I never be recognized by any of my father's acquaintance. I'm doomed if you tell anyone you saw me."

The ravishing teal lips turned up at the corners. "I'm not acquainted with your father, darling. It doesn't count. But did you really make enough to live on that way? No wonder you haven't any gowns worthy of your name."

"I have some older gowns, retrieved from London last fall. As for money . . ." She explained about the allowance, and stressed again how vital it was that her father not learn she had come to London. Her entire future was at the mercy of this strikingly beautiful, bored woman. Would Serephene betray her for a moment's excitement?

The other girl was thinking deeply, but not about that, for she said a moment later, "I'd like to dress you for evening anyway. Humour me, would you? As you may surmise from my current attire—which you must never describe in your fashion columns lest my papa hear of it—I long to design clothing that emphasize a woman's unique nature and personality rather than reinforcing her conformity to the expectations of her class and family."

"Won't your papa hear of it from the crew?"

Serephene's magnificent eyes opened wide again. "Never! They've been my kind protectors since my earliest tottering footsteps. For Papa, you see, has the erratic temper of many creative persons and did not always moderate his language or behavior out of consideration for his children."

Maddie counted herself fortunate for once: her father, stern though he unquestionably was, had resolutely lived up to his clear and oft-stated guiding principles as the head of his household. You always knew where you stood with him.

Her hostess was looking her up and down. "I see you in . . . crimson. Something practical, that you'll feel good in. Silk would pack well, if you're continuing your adventures."

A new silk gown! Whether Serephene's idea of practical would accord with the reality of Maddie's working image remained to be seen, but to say no to a new dress? It could not be done. Maddie nodded.

Serephene sprang to her booted feet, one hand fluffing her teal bustle. "I'll fetch my tape measure and a few lengths of fabric for a pattern. And the most modest gown in my wardrobe for you to wear tonight at dinner. The new one won't be made until we reach London. You will have to see me again to collect it." She surprised Maddie further by clutching her in a fierce hug before dashing out, yelling for her maid.

"Well," said Maddie to TD as she took off her hat at last. "That was unexpected. I do hope she can be trusted. Now, I'm going to take advantage of that library next door to look up old news on those cherished friends of Baron Bodmin, something I have not had time for since this whole affair began. You can fly around in here as long as you hide when someone comes in. These Artificer types would have you apart in a tick-tock to find out how you work, and that secret is not ours to share."

In the library, she settled into one of the pillowy chairs and pushed the blue button. The ceiling panel opened above her, a pole descended, and the monkey climbed down it, hand over paw, just like a living creature. It sat on the wide chair-arm and looked up at Maddie with mischievous brown eyes. A short circus tune jingled. The monkey chortled as it opened its vest with its own paws and demonstrated what each of the buttons did. This was far more capable machinery than any public monkey. Clearly Artificer families kept the best creations for themselves.

After a bit of playing around with the controls,

Maddie came up with every mention of Colonel Muster in the past six months. The sum total of reports confirmed what she already knew: he was retired, he gambled, he spent Christmas in Cairo, and he'd vanished from London around the time the baron's airship was found. Searches for Mrs. Midas-White brought nothing beyond the report that had so infuriated Maddie. For the professors she found just two articles, a week apart, showing their bad blood still simmering. Both articles were published before the baron's body came ashore.

The University Times

WINDY BROWN GASSING AGAINST PROFESSOR PLUMB

A new wrinkle arose in the mysterious case of the missing baron, when American Windsor Jones leveled a public accusation at Professor Polonius Plumb of Cambridge for the theft of his research into the fabled Eye of Africa mask.

Interviewed at the Royal Air Arms Club in London, where he has visiting-veteran privileges, Jones stated, "We both attended the same conference in New York City. We came to England on the same airship. He was in my stateroom for drinks. I showed him the map I'd worked out from years of studying tribal legends. I put it into my book trunk right in front of him, and next day the whole trunk had vanished. As soon as I heard that baron guy was on the trail of the Eye of Africa, I knew the prof had shanghai'd my research for him. When I catch up to Plumb, I'll fix him good. And if that baron makes it back alive, I'll punch him right in the schnoz!"

Professor Plumb, not unexpectedly, had proclaimed his innocence.

The Goggles Grapevine

EVIL EYE DIAMOND GLOWS RED SAYS PROF

Scotland Yard today confirmed there is no case against Professor Polonius Plumb for the theft of Windy Jones' trunk. "Our only possible witness to any sale has gone missing," said Chief Inspector Snidely Bellows. "You know, that chap whose airship was just found floating off the South Coast. Without him or the trunk, we've got nothing."

Plumb proclaimed his innocence and demonstrated his expert knowledge with a long, technical explication of the geological processes by which other rare minerals are compressed into the midst of a diamond to form a so-called 'bloodshot diamond' such as that rumoured to be part of the Eye of Africa mask.

"As for it glowing red when touched by an evil man's blood, that's likely a trick of refracted light when the mask is held at the proper angle."

When the American academic's threat was quoted to him, Plumb said, "Jones yearns to discredit me because I held out for his expulsion from Oxford after that disgraceful incident. If he dares lay a violent hand on me, I'll have him up on charges. Immediately after a sharp lesson in British pugilism."

The professor is departing today for Bodmin Manor in Cornwall. While awaiting news of his friend's fate, he intends to catalogue the baron's papers for his university.

If anything of Jones' was found with Baron Bodmin's papers, Plumb's reputation would be sunk. Maybe that's why Plumb was on his way to Cornwall: to destroy any evidence connecting him with the theft. He was at least temporarily out of Maddie's reach. Jones was who knew where, and Colonel Muster likely dead in some lonely wood, or wherever old soldiers went to die. If Mrs. Midas-White didn't give an interview, there was no avenue in London to avail Maddie's journalistic aspirations. She could only hope Madame had a lead for her about the imposter, or she had thrown away her entire newspaper career and risked her father's wrath for nothing at all.

The lovely pale teal gown Serephene sent in for her to wear to dinner did little to cheer her despite its modish tulle neckline and the intricate leaf-work swooping around the skirt.

Forty hours later, Maddie was in London, saying goodbye to the excited nieces and to Serephene. In addition to the evening gown, the latter had unearthed last Season's conservative blue walking suit from her older sister's wardrobe on board, and insisted on Maddie taking it to match the blue hat "with the bird on it." Thus Maddie was modishly prepared for England, and could walk into a professional women's hostelry in London with her head high.

But not Claridge's Hotel. Both outfits looked a

smidge too much like her old self for that. Conveyed to Paddington Station in an Aquatiempe steam coupe that wove through traffic faster than any horse-drawn coach could manage, she checked her luggage for the day and walked the few blocks to Brooks Mews at the rear of the hotel. The staff entrance was busy, with maids and footmen, cooks and porters all popping in and out. She followed a pretty maid in a black dress and starched white cap to the maids' dressing room. It was the work of moments to find a uniform from a rack, an apron from a shelf, and a cap from the stand beneath the room's only mirror. Stuffing notebook and journalist card into the uniform pocket, and stashing her hat, suit, and handbag far back on an upper shelf, she settled TD into her cleavage and drew up the apron's bib to hide him. Then she followed the clatter of pots to the kitchens.

"Beggin' your pardon, sir," she said to the first waiter she saw. "My mistress would like a coffee tray brought up for her visitors. Where can I get one?"

"New, are you? This way." He hustled past her to a long row of brass cylinders along one wall. Beneath them were open metal racks containing coffee and tea services on trays. "Coffee from the black handles. Brown handles are tea. Cream and milk in the ivory and white. Mind your hands when the steam first releases."

"Yes, sir. Thank you, sir." She fitted up a tray with two cups and started up the back stairs, dodging footmen as they hurried down. On every guest floor, she knew from previous stays, there was a butler's pantry, where the kitchen dumbwaiter brought hot meals up, and each one had a listing of that floor's occupants. She would soon locate Mrs. Midas-White.

Starting on the first guest floor with its airships-in-flight woven carpets, she scanned the butler's blackboard. No Midas-White. She hurried up the servants' stair to the next floor. As she stepped out onto the cog-and-gear carpet there, a woman dressed all in black, from button-boots to veiled hat, left the ascender opposite. Maddie kept her eyes down and hurried toward the butler's pantry, only to hear the woman call out.

"Maddie?"

Maddie kept walking.

"Madeleine Main-Bearing. Does your father know where you are?"

Chapter Nine

FROM BEHIND MADDIE came a peculiar whistle. Her bosom fluttered. Literally fluttered, as TD tried to scramble out from her apron. He chirped, loud and distinctly out of place in the stately hotel's corridor. With both hands on the coffee tray, she could neither stop him nor shush him. She could only hurry away.

When TD reached the top of the apron, he launched himself back down the corridor. Maddie turned. The little bird had landed on the woman in black's shoulder and was rubbing his bronze beak against the veiled cheek. He would only do that for one person.

"Madame Taxus-Hemlock?"

"Yes, dear." Madame subdued TD with a touch on his cocked head. "Come along to my parlour. Unless you really have taken a job here, in which case deliver the coffee first."

"I can fetch more any time." Maddie followed

along the gear-patterned carpet to a large corner suite. Madame unlocked the door and held it for her to pass through into the small foyer. On one side was a large parlour, with a steam-grate set into the old hearth, a pair of wing chairs before it, and a dining area besides. On the other side a door into Madame's bedchamber stood ajar. Maddie set down the tray. "Coffee?"

"Please." Madame released TD as her own Birdie, a swallow twice TD's size, zoomed in from the bedchamber to meet his little compatriot. The two clockworks whizzed around the ceiling fan together, swooped through the plumes in a tall vase, and soared up to perch on a curtain rod from which they could eye the coffee tray. Madame sat by the hearth and accepted a cup and saucer.

Maddie poured her own coffee, liberally sweetened. "Obie said you were in Frankfurt for the dueling. Did anybody die this year?"

"You know we discourage dueling to the death in these enlightened times. Novice rules only. Less exciting but far safer for modern young ladies. Now, tell me everything about your investigations. I've had only Mr. O'Reilly's brief reports to gauge your progress."

Maddie sat opposite and summarized for Madame her final week in Cairo, beginning with Baron Bodmin's disappearance and going on to the discovery that the widow had fled Egypt with both the merchant's jewels and her own visiting cards. The baron's confirmed death and Colonel Muster's disappearance got a mention in context of her thwarted byline dream.

"After all this upheaval, I have no byline and

possibly no job at all. I must find that woman and induce her to stop using my name. Obie said you had investigated her time in Venice; do you know her real name yet?"

"Ah, Maddie. Reckless as ever, I see." Madame smiled at her. "As it happens, the family has watched that young woman intermittently for three years. Her most-used first name is Sarah, and she is very good at disappearing. I daresay she never leaves a place on a loss, either. She has not yet attempted any actions against the family, and we've seen no reason to interfere."

If they had seen reason, Maddie was doubtful Sarah—she had a name at last, unlikely though it was to be her original one—would still be roaming free. "Why were you watching her at all?"

"We considered employing her. She reminds me of me, in my wild youth, save that I used my talents for my family, and occasionally for my government, while she appears to work for her own benefit alone, or occasionally for a client. Once you had placed her time in Cairo for us, we determined from her message trail that she had been informing on Baron Bodmin for an American lady, a Mrs. Midas-White."

"The owner of the White Sky Line? Why, that's the baron's bilked investor. But where did Sarah go when she left the hotel in January? Not to Venice, for another month."

"She communicated from a postal outlet in Cairo, as I recall, but where she resided, I have no information."

Maddie sat back. "Returned to wherever she had lived before the baron's arrival, I suppose, and under some other name. And now to find she was working for Mrs. Midas-White all along. I was headed for that lady's suite when you appeared."

"For what purpose?"

"I hope she'll allow me an interview about the baron. I may not retain my job if I don't present something newsworthy very soon."

"Go ahead then. TD can stay here until your return. And perhaps by that time we will have other avenues to pursue."

Feeling ever so much more confident with Madame's considerable resources at her back, Maddie drained her coffee cup and wondered, briefly, if it was worth going downstairs for another tray. Instead, she smoothed her apron, slid a "Miss Hatter, Fashionista" card from her pocket, and wrote across the back in an orderly copperplate, "Miss Hatter requests the pleasure of an interview at"— she checked the handsome timepiece on Madame's sideboard—"four o'clock today." That would allow her time to retrieve her own clothing from downstairs and present herself as a professional woman. Wealthy people did not, as a rule, notice a servant's facial features, and with the added distraction of a large hat during her journalistic reincarnation, Maddie felt confident she would escape detection.

Soon she was back in the butler's pantry. The rich American had the corner suite opposite from Madame's. She filched a silver salver from the pantry and presented her card at the suite door.

"A lady sent up this card," she said to the tight-lipped maid who opened the door. The woman took the tray into the parlour.

Via a large mirror over the narrow hall table,

Jayne Barnard

Maddie got her first look at the baron's wealthy investor. Mrs. Midas-White was a small woman, dressed for daytime in an elaborately embroidered, white-on-white suit with an immense hooped skirt, completed by a scalloped and pearled hem, neckline, and cuffs. Pearls the size of grapes hung on her ears and throat. Her fingers, clutching Maddie's card, were covered by worked golden sheaths of Byzantine complexity, featuring Baroque pearls, platinum filigree, and bronze points sharpened and cruelly curved to resemble the claws of a very large cat. The claws shredded the card effortlessly, scattering the pieces on the carpet by her chair.

"You know I don't see journalists," she snapped. "Send her away." Then, while the sour maid gathered up the scraps, her mistress glared at someone out of sight. "So you'll do it?"

Maddie shifted to see directly into the parlour. Before the steam grate stood a large man in a camel-hair topcoat finished with both a shoulder cape and a wide astrakhan collar of some chocolate-hued fur. In the mirror above the mantle, he was admiring his extravagant orange moustaches, carefully waxed and shaped into antlers on either side of a small, pink mouth. Did he notice her beyond the doorway? No. He merely stroked a finger along one hairy arabesque with a satisfied smile.

"Fear not, Madame Midas-White," he proclaimed. "I, Hercule Hornblower, will proceed to this baron's remote estate and recover for you the fabled treasure for which you have paid already. No Eye shall remain unseen by Hercule Hornblower." He stroked the other side of his moustaches and added, "I will require an advance against traveling expenses, unless you prefer to deliver me yourself?"

"I do not travel with the hired help."

Hornblower merely held out his hand in unmistakable expectation of payment.

The sour maid returned to the foyer. Dusting the shreds of visiting card into a wastebasket, she said, "My mistress will not see the lady," and ushered Maddie out to the corridor.

The genteel click of the closing door was the knell of Doom. With the weight of failed hopes dragging behind her, Maddie plodded along the gear-patterned carpet to Madame's suite, tapped, and entered. Madame looked up from her newspaper with an inquiring air.

"No good," Maddie told her. "She tore up my card."

"You were gone longer than needed for that."

"I was listening. Mrs. Midas-White, presuming the baron to have found the Eye of Africa mask, has hired a man to find it. A large Frenchman named Hornblower."

"Fabulous moustaches?"

Maddie nodded.

Madame said, "Hercule Hornblower. A celebrated cerebral sleuth. But a Belgian, my dear. Don't call him a Frenchman if you don't wish to make an enemy. Did you chance to overhear where he plans to start?"

"At Bodmin's estate. Cornwall, I think." Maddie slumped into a chair. "Failing an interview with Mrs. Midas-White, I suppose I might pay my own way to Cornwall and interview the baron's staff. Perhaps he did go home first, and hide the mask there, and they just don't like to say before they've had a chance to search for it themselves. What a scoop that would be."

"Indeed," said Madame. "They would not be the only ones searching. Sir Ambrose Peacock was on his way there as well. But perhaps his new wife won't stay in Cornwall when the London Season is beginning."

"His wife? When did he marry?"

"I saw a notice, back in March, I think," said Madame. "Is it important?"

"It might be enlightening to know where he was when his uncle fell overboard. Absence from his brand-new wife would be significant." Poor Clarice, pining for a fashionable fribble who, far from hurrying to her in Cairo, had married someone else.

"I will have someone check Sir Ambrose's itinerary. If to Cornwall you must go—and I daresay it will be safer for you than lurking in London where your papa might run across you any day—then why not let Mrs. Midas-White pay for it?"

"How? She won't even see me."

"She saw the famous detective. I've heard he hates taking notes or writing reports, although I calculate his new employer will expect many. If I were to write you a suitable reference, you could scuttle around to his lodging and get hired on as his secretarial assistant for the trip to Cornwall. What name will you travel under this time? And what colour shall we dye your hair and eyebrows?"

Chapter Ten

WHILE HER NEW boss burbled and snored through his fabulous moustaches, Maddie gazed out at the land unspooling below the wheezing little airship's keel. Bodmin Moor was high, rocky, and, in mid-April, shimmering green even under the scudding gray of yet another rainy day. The airship, a local from Exeter, had too little power to labour high above the rising land, and had not even a coffee service to while away the final hour of their journey from London. What a mercy they'd been able to snatch a bite during the changeover from the London-Exeter shuttle. Even that was a long time after the early breakfast in Madame's suite.

Madame was, indeed, a miracle worker. Not only had her references so impressed the great detective that he hired Maddie on the spot, but she had arranged a room overnight in Claridge's. A pair of staid ladies' shirtwaists in dark blue, which with

Maddie's newly purple hair changed her colouring considerably, arrived after dinner. Then, while Madame cleaned sand from TD's joints and gears, Maddie wrote up her piece on the nieces' Court Presentation gowns. She back-dated it, hoping CJ would assume it was written before she fled Cairo. Did he know yet she had left?

At one point she looked up to see TD's little head tipped straight backward while Madame twisted a slender brass implement down into his neck. Birdie looked on with encouraging twitters. Madame glanced over at Maddie, her deep violet eye magnified horrifically by an oculus five separate lenses thick.

"I am activating a few more of his skills for you. They were not needed in the life of a fashion reporter, but as an investigative reporter you may require them. The usual commands for images and voices, followed by 'at your discretion,' will collect images when there is movement and sounds when someone speaks, for up to several hours."

"Marvelous! So he is now as talented as your Birdie?"

Birdie squawked.

"She did not mean it, dear," said Madame to the clockwork. "Let us rather say, Maddie, that he benefits from Birdie's longer proximity to my toolkit. He will serve you well."

"I meant to ask you about having him painted to blend in better with local birds, as Obie's Tweetle-C does. But perhaps when I settle in my next job, whatever that is."

Madame nodded. "Eventually. Enameling is a tricky process, so as not to disturb the very delicate inner mechanisms. One drop in the wrong crack and a whole system could be jammed up permanently. You remember old Poppa, who could barely move his wings?" Oh, yes, that clumsy old parrot. He might not fly but he could walk and climb, and swore more fluently than any airship pirate. "Enameling many years ago froze his pinion gears. He lives at the Experimental Airship Division with my cousin, cussing out the Admirals whenever one ventures near. I'm surprised they haven't ordered his voice-box removed."

The late tea tray had arrived when a brown hawk landed on Madame's windowsill. Maddie hurried to open the glass. Birdie sat communing with the hawk while TD looked on with his head cocked, as if trying to overhear a message not meant for him. When the hawk left, Birdie hopped over to his mistress.

"Speak," said Madame, and the bird, in a man's voice, reported, "Per Madame's query, Sarah name-unknown is whereabouts unknown. Colonel Muster is not in London; whereabouts unknown. Sir Ambrose Peacock is not in London; listed location Bodmin Manor, Cornwall. Professor Plumb is not in Cambridge; listed location Bodmin Manor, Cornwall. Professor Windsor Jones is not in Oxford; whereabouts unknown. Sir Ambrose Peacock marriage abroad reported in society pages, date unspecified but approximately mid-March; lady's maiden name unlisted. End report."

"Probably a rich tradesman's daughter," said Madame. "I don't know that this was much help after all. At least you will know who you're facing at Bodmin Manor. Is Sir Ambrose or Professor Plumb a risk to your identity?"

"I've not met Sir Ambrose that I recall, and only met Professor Plumb a handful of times around Shepheard's Hotel at Christmas. He has no reason to remember me."

"As well to be sure," said Madame. "I will keep my people alert for slippery Sarah, and inform you promptly if the Honourable Madeleine Main-Bearing is heard of anywhere you are not. Off you go to bed now. You have an early start and a long day tomorrow."

Thus ended a day that had begun over Paris in a state of considerable worry and ended with a new job, new clothing, and a new crack at the twisty Baron Bodmin story. The final article she'd filed last night had concerned Mrs. Midas-White hiring Hercule Hornblower to investigate the baron's demise. If CJ bought that article, he would surely print more items from Cornwall, byline or no byline. What WAS a good byline for an investigative reporter? A pair of initials rather than a first name would keep her gender off the public perception. W.Y. Worthington had a reliable feel, but would any reader grasp that W might stand for Who, What, When, or Where?

Chapter Eleven

MADDIE WAS STILL pondering her byline on the airship over Cornwall as she watched the scenery unfold below. The dawn-tinted rooftops of London had given way to the Green Belt, under which lay the vast steam-driven mansions of Maddie's father and his peers. Beyond them were the home farms and villages of the Old Nobility, mingling here and there with the personal aerodromes of the lesser Steamlords. Lakes, woods, railway lines, and towns had passed under their keel during the long morning.

Hornblower had fallen instantaneously asleep three times by her count, once in the middle of their hurried meal in Exeter. Then he had simple gone off quietly, in whatever position he happened to be, and come back as quietly. Now he was snuffling and grunting in his sleep, annoying her if not the other six passengers, who appeared to be mostly of the clerical classes. No wonder he had said to her, very firmly, that she must observe everything and write down every word concerning any of his investigations. He could not be sure he would be awake to hear or see things for himself. Not that he was missing much on this dawdling journey over the moors. If only he were a quiet sleeper . . .

This tiny local airship, their second transport of the day, floated above green and treeless lands intersected by ancient stone walls. Mine-houses dotted the landscape, their ancient stones surmounted by metallic machinery that sent flumes of steam and gasses as high as the airship flew. A village came in sight, comprised of ten small houses and a church built of local rock. A sprawling, stone building with a mooring mast anchored the opposite end of the village. The airship was so low she could almost make out its sign, swinging in a light breeze. Jamaica Inn. She nudged the great detective, who sat up with a start.

The only suggestion of a rooftop terminal was a narrow wooden walkway extending a few feet from one gabled end of the building. Surely the airship was not so maneuverable as to line up to that frail-looking gangplank? It took two passes but the gangplank and the airship's exit did line up. They were hooked together for safety, and the half-dozen passengers shuffled cautiously across to a small rooftop doorway while their luggage was winched down to the cobbled courtyard.

Inside the roof gable, the stairs were so narrow that Maddie's skirt brushed both sides, and she feared her larger employer might not pass that way at all. But, with only a few grunts and mutters, he arrived at the inn's lobby and stood brushing dusty spiderwebs off his camel-hair topcoat while he looked about. Maddie looked too. Hanging lanterns drooped from aged beams, casting an oily glow over the dark room and the longer, darker barroom beside it. The paneling was black with centuries of coal smoke from three vast fireplaces. No clean steam boiler here.

Hercule Hornblower demanded of the innkeeper, "A steamer, good man, for Bodmin Manor." The innkeeper eyed him stolidly, jaws working on something that might be a hunk of gristle or a plug of tobacco. "Did you not hear me? At once!"

After a few more chews, the man said, "Can't."

"Of course you can. Why would you not? A steamer, I say, and quickly. Do you not know who I am?"

The innkeeper's face said he didn't care. Maddie, with visions of a cold bed in a dark and possibly haunted inn, hurried over.

"Please, sir, we are very anxious to be on our way. If there is no steamer available, is there another conveyance we might hire?"

After a moment's consideration, the innkeeper nodded. "Horse-drawn."

As Hercule Hornblower drew himself up, Maddie said hurriedly, "We'll take it, thank you. How soon may we depart?"

"Soon's it's back from Launceston and the horses rested." The man hawked into a conveniently placed spittoon and then, anticipating the next question, added, "Half hour, maybe more. I'll fetch ye in time. Ladies' parlour that way." One heavy hand pointed to a passage that led away from the bar.

Hornblower followed Maddie to a snug room, fitted out with heavy wooden furniture of surprisingly modern design. The armchairs bulged under bold tartan coverings, carved feet peeking from beneath pleated skirts. The lamps and tables bore ruffled covers, while incidental cushions were stuffed to bursting their buttons. The aged walls were brightened by prints of rosy-cheeked children playing in picturesque cottage gardens. A scattering of newspapers lay on the table. Hornblower, after examining his moustaches in the speckled mirror over the hearth, lowered his bulk onto a sofa and reached for the top paper in the stack, ignoring his new minion.

Maddie prowled the small room, stretching her legs, until a maid came in with a tea tray and the day's newspapers, fresh off the airship still floating above the inn. Accepting a cup and saucer, she refused an elderly biscuit, and reached for the top newspaper, a Kettle Conglomerate publication. If CJ had seen fit to print the articles she submitted last night, it would signify his forgiveness. But Hornblower grabbed the paper first, flipping through at speed until he found something he had apparently been seeking. He read silently and then flung the paper onto the floor.

"Bah. They have again used the incorrect image. How many times have I, the greatest detective now in England, explained to them that the uniform of the Belgian police is no longer appropriate? How many times has Hercule Hornblower's image been sent to them with a strongly worded letter? But no. They use the old image." He stamped one weighty foot. The tea service shivered. As he sat back, he added with calm curiosity, "I wonder who told them I had taken the case of the baron and the missing mask. I would have done it myself but my moustaches needed to be trimmed before the journey."

He did not sound displeased at the publicity, only at the photograph. When his attention turned to the next paper in the fresh pile, Maddie collected the discarded one from the carpet and skimmed the article. Of course, no by-line, but the words were hers:

Famed Belgian investigator Hercule Hornblower has been hired by Mrs. Midas-White, the American investor left most financially bereft by Baron Bodmin's untimely end. His tasks are two: to learn the manner of the baron's death, and to find the Eye of Africa mask if the baron had succeeded in returning it to England before his demise.

[Here appeared Hornblower's declaration from his meeting with Mrs. Midas-White on the previous afternoon, as close as Maddie could remember it, followed by a description of his fashionable overcoat and the attention he paid to his moustaches.]

With the confidence of many solved cases behind him and the good will of Scotland Yard to uphold him, Hornblower is en route to Bodmin Manor in pursuit of Truth. Our reporter will send daily updates on his progress.

Maddie returned to her teacup and drank thankfully. A pittance for the short item, to be sure, but any item that ended in "daily updates" signified

CJ would continue to print whatever she could send him from Cornwall, so long as it related to the mystery of the baron's death and was presented in a sufficiently sensationalist style to thrill the readers of his various broadsheets. Do well in this, and he might even assign her other mysteries when this one was solved.

The maid, returning to collect the tea tray, shyly offered a tattered periodical to Maddie. "It's a few months old now, Miss, but all the society gossip and a lovely article on the daring stockings ladies wore in Egypt last winter. Embroidered with snakes and other heathen patterns about the ankle, they say." Since Maddie had written about the stockings herself, she thanked the girl and said she had better read some local doings instead, to familiarize herself with the place. "Well, Miss, if you will step upstairs with me, then, for we clips the best of the local news and sets them in frames. I'll show you."

She led the way, not to the narrow stairs for the airship dock, but to a wider flight, built square around a supporting pillar. Up to a landing they went, on which the paneling could hardly be seen beneath crowded, cheap frames over yellowing newsprint.

Maddie scanned the headlines while her guide chattered, and glimpsed a familiar face: Baron Bodmin himself, posed outside a mansion of local stone in the garb of an African explorer, from his pale khaki shooting jacket to his gleaming white pith helmet. The article below was boilerplate about his departure on a great quest for a wondrous treasure. A smaller photo showed his airship, the *Jules Verne*, bobbing above a slate-tiled roof, with the baron in his pith helmet and another man, his features indistinct, both waving from the cockpit. The caption beneath was lost under the edge of the frame.

"This one." Maddie pointed. "Do you know the name of that man with Baron Bodmin?"

"Yes, Miss. That's Captain, no, Colonel Muster, a great friend of the baron's. He was there when the baron left, being in charge of shutting up the house for his friend. Just think: he slid down a single rope to the roof after this image was taken. A daring gentleman. He had medals." She nodded solemnly.

"You haven't an article about the baron's airship being found adrift?"

"Oh, yes, Miss. We have a whole wall of them in the long bar. Every newspaper that came, my master clipped out the whole page. Bought special frames and all. The poor baron. What a sad end to his great adventure."

"Did he come here after his return, before he was found in the sea?" The girl worked that out, then shook her head. Ah, well, it was a long shot anyway.

As Maddie turned away, the maid volunteered, "No. He only sent over a telegram."

"A telegram?" Maddie launched an even longer shot. "Do you know what it said?"

"Course I do. It's hanging up behind the desk in the lobby, being the last words of our own moor's baron. He said, or wrote really—the housekeeper's boy brought over the form—HOME STOP SUCCESS STOP COME AT ONCE TO ADVISE NEXT STEPS STOP STOP STOP."

Success?

He had found the mask.

What a coup if Maddie could prove the mysterious mask had reached England. She might even find it at Bodmin Manor. "When was this telegram sent? How many days before the airship was found drifting?"

"Three?" the girl said hesitantly. "Is that important?"

"Are you sure it was three?"

She nodded. "The housekeeper's boy, he brought me a note from my sweetheart, too, inviting me to a dance. Same day as airship blowed in, the dance were, and me with a new hem to set in between. All of three days and no mistake, Miss."

"Thank you. You have been most helpful." Maddie slipped a coin into the maid's hand. "If you'll show me that telegram form?"

Leading her down to the lobby, the girl took the framed telegraph form from the wall and held it out toward Maddie. On the hat, TD poked up his head, but the maid appeared not to see the small movement. Nor did she note several slight clicking sounds as Maddie peered closely at the framed flimsy.

"Thank you," said Maddie again, and watched her re-hang the frame. "What's the next one over? About the wedding?" The maid handed it over. It was not a Kettle paper, but one that another consortium printed up for all the airship services in England.

The Foghorn Afloat

ROMANTIC AIRBOARD WEDDING

On his winter's travels on the Continent, Sir Ambrose Peacock lost an uncle but gained a bride. After a romantic meeting in Venice by the Grand Canal, the English knight lost no time in winning his fair lady's hand. They were married aboard an airship en route to Paris, where they enjoyed an idyllic honeymoon until the news of Baron Bodmin's deserted airship reached them.

"I only regret my uncle is not here to meet my bride," said Sir Ambrose, when the pair disembarked at the Jamaica Inn in Cornwall, the closest regular stop to Bodmin Manor. Sir Ambrose's uncle, Baron Bodmin, was on a quest for a fabled Nubian treasure when his airship was found adrift over the English Channel, bringing his newly-wedded heir in haste to the secluded family estate.

In response to questions directed at his lovely new wife, Sir Ambrose replied for her. "Yes, I'm sure she will enjoy living in my isolated manor. I hope my uncle gets declared dead soon so I can sell off a few things." As this reporter turned away, Sir Ambrose grasped a sleeve. *"I don't suppose you could lend me a fiver? My wife and I have excess baggage charges and the airship won't unload our trunks until we pay up."*

So Sir Ambrose had been in Paris when his uncle disappeared. Was he ruthless enough to secretly meet his uncle as the latter sailed over, and throw him to his death before returning to France with the fabled mask? And yet he'd been unabashed in claiming poverty to the reporter, though that could be a ruse to deflect suspicion. What manner of man was he? The accompanying photo showed a slender young dandy in the smartest of London waistcoats and an immense tan top-hat. Beside him, heavily veiled, stood a dainty lady whose hat barely reached his shoulder. The new bride.

The face might be hidden, but Maddie was very sure she recognized that gown. She had described it in intimate detail for a column on clothing worn at Baron Bodmin's farewell party in Cairo. She held the frame up where TD could click an image and then handed it back to the maid.

"Can I send a telegram from here?"

"Yes, Miss. Two bob for the form and whatever the letters adds up to."

"It will go right away?"

"Yes, Miss. Soon's the master steps back inside after telling them to keep the horses in harness."

"Thank you." Maddie took the form, and a pencil, and set in the address line: Madame Taxus-Hemlock at Claridge Hotel London. Below that, concentrating on printing very neatly, she set down the words, "SARAH AT BODMIN AS LADY P STOP HELP STOP STOP STOP."

Exactly what help she wanted she could not have said in that shocked moment of recognition, but apart from the temptation to tackle the imposter on her own, she wanted more than anything to have someone else know the identity of Sir Ambrose Peacock's shy new bride. After all, anything might happen on a lonely moor, and this time, it might not be the mysterious Sarah who vanished when exposure threatened.

Chapter Twelve

JAMAICA INN'S HORSE-DRAWN conveyance was not so much a carriage as a tarted-up farm cart. An aged loveseat was fixed to a dray, half sheltered from the elements by an accordion of oil-canvas canopy that creaked ominously whenever a rain-laden draught tugged at it. Before the cart had climbed the first rocky ridge, the carriage-robe laid across Maddie's knees was chillingly damp. Her feet in their button boots rested on a warmed brick, but her hands, clenched under the robe, cooled rapidly. Hornblower seemed not to feel the cold, but that didn't stop him complaining about the conveyance with every lurch. Why didn't he pick this time to fall asleep?

The clouds crept down, ever closer to the narrow track as it wound upward over the deserted moor. Where was Bodmin Manor exactly, on this mournful emptiness that shared its name?

Along with this question, which grew more

weighty as they crossed each uninhabited vale, another hung in the scales: would Sir Ambrose's new bride, Lady Sarah, recognize Maddie as a threat the instant she arrived? Maddie had not yet determined how to act. The insult of the visiting card was a burning itch, demanding satisfaction. But to challenge one's hostess was to destroy any hope of remaining incognito and retaining one's job, not to mention that vital allowance. Would all the honour left in the world eventually give way to the need for money?

That last was one question too many for Maddie. She pulled the lap robe higher and simply endured until yellow gate-lanterns glimmered through the dusk on the far side of yet another green valley. When at last they stopped in the lee of the gray, stone house, it took all her will to shift her freezing feet. If the lady of the manor offered her a poisoned cup now, she would drink it and gladly, if only it was warm.

She was not put to that test, for Sir Ambrose, greeting them in the central hall, at once made his lady's apologies. "She finds the air of Cornwall enervating, and keeps to her bed most days," he said, his thin hands flapping helplessly. Duty done, he shot like a hunted fox into a doorway on the left, through which Maddie glimpsed a wall of bound books. The voices of at least one other man rumbled from within, asking about the new arrivals.

The footman picked up an oil lamp and led Hornblower up an old oak stair that creaked under every footfall. Maddie followed, more than once snatching back her hand from a clinging cobweb, and trying not to think what might be falling onto her hat from the ancient tapestries that dangled from unseen rafters. Her bedchamber was no more salubrious. A small fire sulked on the hearth, belching earthy smoke into the room. She felt the bedding and determined to demand a warming pan from the next maid or housekeeper to put in an appearance.

No-one appeared, however, and eventually she draped the bedding over the room's two chairs to air and dry, as close to the fire as she dared leave it. Then she, with her black notebook, a hand-light, and TD in separate pockets, crept back down the stairs to explore the home of the legendary adventurer, Baron Bodmin.

The library, for such it obviously was, was deserted under a few hanging lamps. Darkened and crackled portraits hung from fraying wire over the mantle and between the windows. Along the shelves, in the intervals of bound volumes, were curios brought from distant corners of the world: sextants and globes, chunks of ore from which mineral flecks gleamed, bone fish-hooks and ivory netsuke, carnival masks, and innumerable devices of gears, gauges, and lenses whose purposes she could not divine. From the used glasses and overflowing ashtrays, as well as the warmth of its fire, the room was in general use by the men in residence. A likely spot to overhear something of interest, then; she looked about for places where TD might be concealed amongst the clutter.

A door near the hearth led to a gloomy parlour. Maddie switched on her hand light and, by its green glow, looked around. This room had a feminine décor, with cloisonné boxes (all empty), painted miniatures of children, and a workbasket containing more cobwebs than needlework. The small aluminum seam-crawlers in it were clearly of an earlier era, the thread spools on their backs too faded to determine their original colours. The room was dingier and much colder than the library. Clearly the new mistress of the house had not made it her own. And yet someone had been here recently, for there were signs of a heavy skirt trailing in the dust along the fireplace wall, and wider smudges near some of the furnishings. An archway led to the hall, shielded by a painted screen and velvet draperies too dirty to reveal their hue.

Shivering in the chill damp, Maddie hurried back to the library for a quick search through the large writing desk. One drawer yielded blank telegram forms identical to the one framed at Jamaica Inn. She stuffed several into her notebook for future use. The other drawers held various items of stationery equipment, but nothing of interest. Wherever Baron Bodmin had kept his secrets, it was not this desk. When the dinner gong went, she hurried across the hall and found the dining room already occupied.

By Colonel Muster, still wearing the suspiciously dark lenses she remembered from Egypt.

Chapter Thirteen

THE COLONEL WAS not abroad "for his health," as his family would doubtless prefer.

Not dead by his own hand, as the regiment he lately disgraced would prefer.

Not in London paying off his debts, as his landlady and others would prefer, although his natty attire implied he was not entirely without funds, or credit.

He was simply hiding out from irate creditors at his old friend's isolated manor.

Had he been there the whole time since fleeing London?

He did not recognize her, for he merely stood up until she was seated and then dropped into his chair again without the slightest attempt at conversation.

Professor Plumb appeared soon after, unmistakable in his Oriental smoking gown and his fez from the Cairo medina. Behind him came Hercule Hornblower, holding forth on the subject nearest to his heart, namely his own comfort. Or the lack thereof, for there was much to complain of at Bodmin Manor. Once again, he fell asleep in mid-sentence. How had he ever made his name as a great detective, when he put his own comfort ahead of questioning and observing? Sir Ambrose joined them and apologized once more for his wife's absence.

Relieved of her worry over confrontation with Sarah and the resulting exposure of her Egyptian persona, which would make her investigations here impossible to pursue, Maddie savoured the aromas of roasted beef and a claret sauce being brought in by a sturdy housekeeper and the footman from earlier. No ceremony was observed; dishes passed from hand to hand without conversation, and she fell to eating as rapidly as the men did, waiting for a chance to break the ice, or for Hornblower to seize the opportunity to grill the men closest to the deceased baron. He said nothing, but took seconds of everything, while she seethed with impatience. Would that she could question them herself! When they'd all slaked their first hunger, she would make the attempt.

She was thwarted. Hardly had she set down her utensils when the housekeeper, with a truncated curtsey, informed her coffee would be brought to her in the ladies' parlour while the gentlemen were at their port. She rose, thinking there must be another parlour, but the woman led her across the hall to the dark, cold room and there left her, with a candelabra for company.

Slipping through the library door, she placed TD on a cluttered shelf and whispered, "Listen for me.

At your discretion."

As men's voices sounded in the hall, she retreated to the parlour, drew the door mostly shut, and studied the swirls on the floor. It looked almost as if someone in a long skirt had knelt by that sofa and reached underneath, but for what purpose? Cleaning had definitely not been the objective. Nobody had cleaned here for many years.

When the housekeeper returned, she was seated in a hastily brushed chair by the empty grate, wondering if she wouldn't be better off just going to bed. The woman set down her coffee and said, "Sorry, miss, that I didn't get up to tend you when you arrived. There's only me to do the supper, see, and the house hasn't half gone to shambles since the old mistress passed away. Master didn't care for women about the house, even to clean it."

At last an opportunity for questions. Maddie seized it, but with little gain. The baron had not summoned his housekeeper on his return from foreign parts, although she was just a step away on her brother's small farm, and she was as shocked as anyone when he washed up dead on a beach five miles away. She had not returned to Bodmin Manor until sent for by Sir Ambrose last week. As the gentlemen could now be heard in the library, she cast a nervous glance over her shoulder.

Despite the urgings of curiosity, Maddie dropped her inquisition rather than be overheard. With no chance of retrieving TD until the library emptied, she asked for a warming pan and went up to her bedchamber. There, she remade her bed and laid out her thickest nightgown. With a second candle ruthlessly filched from Hornblower's room next door, she wrote for him a brief report, the gist of which was "nobody said anything during supper." Then she set down her impressions of the manor in an atmospheric item for CJ. On the morrow, if she learned nothing of more substance to add, she would seek the boy who carried messages, and send him back to the inn with a telegraph form.

Maddie dozed in her bed for some time before she heard Hercule Hornblower stumbling and grumbling beyond the wall. She soon remembered TD hidden in the library and, pausing only to don her dressing gown and shoes, set off to fetch him. In the pale glow of her hand light, she crept along the upper hall and down the creaky stairs. The lower hall was filled with shadow. The ancient house creaked and whispered in the dark. Again she thought of large spiders spinning their dusty webs down to catch her hair, and shuddered.

The library door stood ajar. By the glow of a dying fire within, she avoided the furnishings and found the shelf where she had left the little bird. He came forward, cold to her touch, and wrapped his little bronze claws around her finger. She cradled him with a murmur and turned away, only to see a faint gleam under the closed parlour door. Somebody was in there.

Out to the hall she and TD went, and along to the dusty velvet curtain. Beyond it, a woman's shadow bobbed in the light of a lone candle as she felt along a wall, the sleeve of her thick dressing gown brushing it clean panel after panel. She shifted a wing chair and knelt behind it, and when she came up again, Maddie saw her face.

Lady Sarah Peacock was not so much ill every day

as tired out from searching all night.

Maddie held TD up to the edge of the painted screen, hoping his new optical settings could penetrate the dimness. At last something to report to Hercule Hornblower tomorrow, if he could stay awake long enough to listen.

Chapter Fourteen

IN THE MORNING Maddie woke to a thundering on her bedchamber door. She stumbled toward it. Hornblower stood there, his moustaches quivering with impatience. The Coast Guard had sent a steamer to bring him to view the baron's body, and he could not go without her to take notes. She scrambled into her clothes, grabbed her notebook, and sent TD to her hat. She had not stayed awake last night to listen to whatever conversation he had collected in the library, and could only hope that whatever she asked him to listen to today would not be erasing those older records with every new word.

Soon she and her empty stomach were jouncing along the rocky track in bright morning sunshine. A breeze sweet with meadow flowers kissed her face. Far away, sunlight danced on the sea. Above a rocky headland bobbed the orange tethered balloon of the Coast Guard Station. The building came into sight, and beyond it, winched right down to the wharf, was the sturdy expeditionary airship she had seen four busy months ago above a Cairo street: the *Jules Verne*.

Thrilled to meet the famous London detective, the Coast Guard officer ordered the *Jules'* gangplank run out and led them up it. The small airship wobbled a bit as they stepped aboard, but seemed still air-worthy despite its adventures. Gazing around avidly, Maddie wished Obie were here to give the working parts a once-over. Although not an airship engineer, he knew enough to tell if some vital cog had irretrievably broken.

The airship's interior was one long cabin. A hammock dangled from the central beam, with two chests open below it. One showed a jumble of hard-worn clothing, the other a biscuit tin, a jar of preserved apricots, and a bent fork. Spartan rations indeed. Two chairs were set on squat posts bolted to the floor; they could be spun toward a small table or the windows or the instrument panel at the bow. On the table were a spirit stove and a single, used glass. Another glass had smashed on the floor nearby. Hornblower did not appear to notice it, but Maddie leaned far over and, under the pretense of holding her hat, touched TD to signal an image.

"This," said the duty officer, "is what really got our attention."

Maddie looked along his pointing arm. In the window directly above the instrumentation panel was a small, round hole. She walked forward, stopping with one foot in the air rather than step on an ominous dark stain in the worn floorboards.

"Is that—?" she asked.

"Dried blood. Yes, we think so. Have you seen enough here, Mr. Hornblower, sir? I sent for the coroner directly we got your message, and he will be waiting to explain the remains to you." He led the way from the airship, with the great detective in ponderous thought behind him. Maddie bent over to capture the image of the stain, and then hurried after.

The coroner waited outside, his sparse, silvery hair blowing in the onshore breeze and his silvery-blue eyes magnified alarmingly by tarnished brass-rimmed goggles. He handed Hornblower down to solid ground and ignored Maddie as he burbled.

"Oh, sir, I can't tell you how eager we are to have you working on our little mystery. This way, sir. My morgue, such as it is, is just below. We have kept the remains cool, and they don't smell near as bad as they did when found. Watch your step coming down, sir. A bit slick from the tide yet."

Talking all the while, he ushered them across a stretch of shingle and into a dim stone cellar below a fish salting plant. He threw open wide boat-doors that faced the water. Reflected sunlight streamed in, bouncing off arrays of mirrors, amplifying itself until it seemed, if possible, brighter than outdoors. In the glare lay Baron Bodmin.

Maddie, expecting a sodden corpse in a state of advanced decay, had her hand up to her nose. But all she smelled was fresh air with an undertone of rotting seaweed. She lowered the glove and looked upon the largely skeletal remains laid out upon a trestle table. They were clad in the rags of a once-elegant brocade smoking jacket over a battered leather waistcoat. Strong cord was lashed around each wrist. Hornblower peered at the body too, saying nothing. From head to foot—only one foot, Maddie noted—and back again he looked.

"You are sure," he intoned, "that these bones are the remains of Baron Bodmin?" He managed to remain alert to finish the sentence, but by then Maddie had begun to recognize the slowed words and slump of the shoulders that preceded his lapses into upright slumber.

"Yes, sir." The coroner, apparently unaware, pulled back the largest scrap of jacket. "See that rib there? I bound that up myself when he fell off a horse as a lad of eight. The right tibia was a flight experiment off a barn, do I recall aright, and this little finger here what's all scarred together? That's from the sound cannon he made to scare the crows off his first little airship. Always peckin' and puncturin' his balloon, they were. It's him, right enough, even weren't he carrying evidence in his pocket."

"Evidence?" Maddie jumped in to cover Hornblower's silence. The coroner pointed to a long bench across the rear of the boat shed. Likely in less grisly times it served for tools. Now it held, first, three papers spread out and held down at the edges by beach rocks, and second, a small trunk tipped on its side. The lid was open to display tight-packed books and papers, only a little wrinkled and mildewed around the perimeter.

Maddie bent over the sea-stained papers, tipping her hat brim to give TD a good line of sight. A laissez-passer from the British Protectorate in Egypt, wrinkled and ink-run, but still recognizable if you'd had one. A similar document printed under the

Empire Explorers Club crest, of no official standing but serving as an introduction to other Explorers wherever encountered. The third was an image from a very good instrument, showing the baron's elegant coat sleeve as he held up a mask.

The mask?

Against the tanned hand, the life-sized mask gleamed darkly. White fragments of shell rimmed its mouth and filled its eyes. Mid-forehead was a chunk of crystal the size of a child's fist, through which a faint light shone from a nearby candelabra. If that was the Eye, and it was truly a diamond rather than a quartz crystal with other mineral intrusions, it was of incalculable value. Maddie took the image over to Hornblower, jostling him gently as she held it out.

"That was taken in the baron's library," she told him. "And what he holds must be the Eye of Africa mask. We should take this image back to the house and see if Professor Plumb can confirm it."

The coroner nodded reluctantly. "Seeing as it's Mr. Hornblower requesting it." He eyed Maddie sternly. "It's still evidence, and you treat it as such."

Wondering how on earth she could become a successful investigative journalist without a man to pretend to be her superior, Maddie placed the image carefully between two blank pages of her black notebook.

From the trunk she selected a hand-drawn map of a dune-marked desert—notable for the initials W and J in the upper right, by the compass rose—and a couple of notebooks. One was mostly undamaged and dealt with legends pertaining to the Eye, while the other, in a different hand and ink, dealt with the provisioning needed for one man for twelve weeks. A cursory glimpse showed the majority of the trunk's contents were written in the first hand. The books were marked with the initials "W.J." There were bits of sand and a few dead insects.

This, she was sure, was the trunk stolen from Professor Windsor Jones on his transatlantic crossing. All his painstaking research, probably a lifetime's accumulation, had gone with the adventurous baron to the Nubian desert, a journey most likely made possible by Professor Plumb's purloining. Then and there she made a vow to never mention again showing Plumb the photograph of the mask, although she did not see how she could prevent his seeing it if Hercule Hornblower commanded it. She turned back to the coroner.

"If he was only in the water at best a few weeks, why was the body so completely stripped of flesh? Surely a longer immersion would be required?"

"Shad," said the coroner. "A couple of big runs a few days apart, eat everything in their path. Seagulls too, they'll eat anything. Maybe they had a peck or two at what was left when he came ashore."

Maddie shuddered. "And his hands were tied to the trunk, if I remember the newspaper reports correctly?"

"Aye."

"Was death caused by drowning, or by the fall into the water?"

"Or . . ." The coroner looked expectantly at Hercule Hornblower, who looked blank. Maddie went back to the corpse. There was something about the skull, a piece actually missing from the back.

"Or perhaps by hitting his head on something in the water?" she asked. The coroner shook his head.

136

She scanned the body again but could find no other wound.

"Allow me." The coroner lifted the skull and tilted it backward in the beam from a mirror. Light flooded the interior. "Look in there."

Fretting with impatience, Maddie had to wait until her boss had looked his fill. He only muttered into his moustaches, leaving, once again, Maddie to ask the questions as they occurred to her.

"Something hit the inside of the skull and forced its way out? How is that possible?"

The coroner nodded. At Hornblower, who had done and said nothing to the point. Was Maddie *invisible*? She set her jaw and leaned in again, turning her head this way and that, and finally saw, on the right eye socket, a tiny chip out of the bone.

"Something went in through the eye and out through the back of his head," she said. Native tribes in the desert might chase off explorers by throwing spears at them. But could their spears be thrown hard enough to pierce a head like this? If one had, how could the baron get all the way back to England, only to die here with no sign of a spear either in his head or on his airship? The hole in the airship window, and the bloodstain there, did not fit either, not unless he'd brought a native all this way with him. Was a native, alive or dead, soon to be found roaming Cornwall? Incredible. "It was a bullet, wasn't it?"

For the first time, the coroner looked at her. "Yes, miss, we think it was."

Maddie could have danced on the spot. She had made a correct deduction and forced this man to acknowledge her. She smiled at him and bent over the skull again, tilting her head to allow TD to record the hole. Hercule Hornblower walked out of the boathouse onto the shingle beach and stood, surveying the pier, the water, and the boats.

Maddie asked the final question. "Where exactly was the body found?"

"You'll need a boat for that, miss. Duty officer up above will be happy to take you along the shore. It's a long trip, so you'll be wanting lunch first. The pub up along the coast road does a nice Shad and chips this season."

Shad? Maddie's hollow stomach flipped right over.

Chapter Fifteen

RETURNING TO BODMIN Manor much later that day, damp all over from sea-spray and particularly chilled about the feet, Maddie saw an airship approaching it from the other direction. The nose of the small craft grew in the sky, bathed pink by the setting sun, until the White Sky logo on the hull was plain to see. Surely only Mrs. Midas-White might requisition a White Sky administrative vessel to go to the wilds of a Cornish moor. Could she not give a full twenty-four hours to her detective without checking up on him?

When the Coast Guard steamer glided onto the uneven paving of the Bodmin Manor forecourt, the owner of the White Sky Line was being lowered to those same stones in a sturdy cage-lift that barely contained her voluminous skirt. A long-tailed traveling coat in a rich chocolate covered much of the skirt's fine tangerine taffeta; both garments were trimmed with combed alpaca wool. The lady's hands, despite the chill of the late afternoon, were bare to the brass claws that glittered in the last sunlight. If she felt the cold at all, she gave no indication, but swept to the front door and pointed to its knocker. The crewman who had escorted her down hurried to pound it.

The steamer, under a nudge from Hornblower, whooshed away to the stable-yard. There Hornblower leaped out like a much younger person, ordered Maddie to write out a fair report of the day for him immediately, and vanished through the kitchen door, leaving her to thank the Coast Guard driver.

She was hurrying toward the house when a small, brown sparrow dropped from the rooftop, barrel-rolled, and landed neatly on her shoulder. It twittered; TD hopped from the hat down to the same shoulder. She put a gloved hand up to hide the pair from eyes in the house, and heard TD mutter in her ear.

"Which is your chamber? Can I reach it from the roof?"

It was Obie's voice, and of course the brown sparrow was TC. How and why they were here she would learn soon enough. Pausing only to count windows across the upper story, she gave the bird the direction. It spiraled upward as she slipped inside the kitchen door.

Her room was as dusty and chilled as she'd left it, although someone had shaken the bedclothes into order. She threw off her hat, unlatched the window, sat down by the cold grate, and began to copy out her day's notes into an official-sounding report. When Obie crawled through the casement she waved him to silence and handed him the first page of the report to read while she completed the second.

"That should do it," she said after a moment. "We now know the mask was in the manor at some point before the baron went into the sea. I wonder, should I tell someone official that Professor Plumb stole Professor Jones' research for the baron, or leave that to Hornblower?"

"Leave it," said Obie. "Jones is booked back to America on my next scheduled voyage; if he hasn't thought to ask the Coast Guard by then, I'll nudge him to telegraph back from the ship."

"All right." Relieved to have an echo for her reluctance to get further involved, she asked, finally, "What brings you here?"

"Dead-headed down thanks to a mate, when I found Mrs. Midas-White was coming. Since I'm on leave, Madame wanted me here to lend an eye on Lady Sarah. Is it really her?"

"Yes. At least, she's the woman I saw in Cairo with the baron. And she was searching the parlour last night, in the dark, tapping for a secret hiding place. Do you suppose Baron Bodmin let something slip to her all those months ago, never thinking she would ever see his moldering manor herself?"

"Men will reveal almost any secret to a woman under the right circumstances." Obie handed back her second page. "Who else is here?"

"Professor Plumb. Sir Ambrose; did Madame tell you Lady Sarah is married to him? Oh, and Colonel Muster, who claims to be in charge of the baron's estate. He looks like he'd dispatch a human with no more consideration than a sparrow." She rubbed TD's beak. "I won't let him near you, little friend."

"It's a far cry from killing in combat to murdering an individual in peacetime," Obie said. "Most go peaceably back to their old life and never harm another soul. Now, this report says the baron was shot through the eye, inside his vessel. Nobody who knew about airships would dare fire a weapon inside that little cockpit. The whole machine could have gone up in a ball of flame."

"Well, somebody did." Maddie held up the sheets of her report side by side for TD to image. "I don't know if Lady Sarah or Sir Ambrose can shoot, or the Professor."

"Jones can. He gave an exhibition off the rear platform on the voyage to England. Hiram said he clipped a playing card at twenty paces in a sea wind. And he shot out the left lens of the second mate's goggles, while they were on his hat. Scorched the hat, but not the hair beneath it. Drunk as a hound, he was."

"Fine shooting indeed. But was he anywhere near Cornwall when Baron Bodmin died?" She clipped the papers together at the corner and shook out her skirts. "I've got to give Hornblower this report right away. Can TC send a copy back to Madame for insurance?"

"Sure thing. I know you too well to think you won't go prowling around in the dark again, so send TD up to our airship if you run into trouble, and I'll jump to your rescue."

"As if I need you to rescue me." Maddie grinned. "Which of us untangled who from that cargo net over Cape Town?"

"One little misstep," said Obie, unabashed. "Mind your step with Lady Sarah. Madame said she's been ruthless, although never killed anyone that the family could discover."

"She'll stay in her room for sure now, rather than risk being spotted by Mrs. Midas-White, her ex-employer."

Maddie's confidence was misplaced. In search of Hercule Hornblower, she found the lady of the house in the library, making polite conversation with Mrs. Midas-White over a tea tray. She stopped in the doorway, stunned to silence by a morass of conflicting emotions at the sight of the woman she had pursued so far from Shepheard's Hotel. Both ladies glanced up, but neither gave any sign of previous acquaintance. Indeed, they appeared to regard each other as strangers too. Curious, if they had worked together over the winter. Likely Sarah had been using some other name then, and perhaps they had not met in person.

Colonel Muster, Professor Plumb, and Sir Ambrose were standing around with teacups, rigid with the discomfort of gentlemen who would rather be elsewhere but can think of no acceptable excuse to flee. Or, in this case, nowhere to flee to, with the library occupied by ladies. Doubly thankful for the precaution that had placed her secretarial oculus firmly over her eye, and for the purple straight hair that had replaced her brown, wavy Cairo coiffeur, Maddie backed out of the room very quickly indeed.

The housekeeper was busy shaking out the little parlour, presumably for the ladies' later use. No retreat there. Hornblower, the footman told her, was in the dining room, having demanded afternoon coffee by himself. She presented the report, snatched a cream bun to make up for refusing the Shad at luncheon, and hurried upstairs with no idea what she would, or could, say when next she was faced with her duplicitous hostess.

Huddled in her coverlet by the cold hearth in her chamber, she listened to the conversations TD had managed to record during his hours in the library on the previous evening.

While Hornblower remained in the room, the talk had been mostly by him. Not questioning his more-or-less captive subjects, but, as usual, talking about himself. A shameless dropper of famous names, he claimed credit for the return of this peer's diamonds and another's kidnapped heir, that merchant's defalcating accountant and this one's overdue steamship. Once he was gone, however, the tenor of the evening shifted. The men's voices came through with intermittent clarity, as they paced the room or moved between their chairs and the drinks cart.

Sir Ambrose was shrill. "She's come to take my entire inheritance. If there's any valuable books or curios, we must hide them. Professor, what's the most valuable?"

Professor Plumb, sounding weary, and maybe a little drunk. "Nothing in this dust-heap is worth a plugged farthing."

The pair explored that theme to the point of tedium before Plumb, losing patience, snapped, "If you want to know where his money went, ask Muster. Same place as the pile he won from you, I shouldn't wonder. Once a gambler, always a gambler."

"I didn't gamble with Bodmin. He was my friend." The colonel couldn't be bothered to sound offended.

Sir Ambrose made up for it. "You wouldn't win his

money but you would mine? So I'm not your friend? I should throw you out of my house then."

"It's not yours until the estate's settled, little rooster. As the executor, I control that timeline. Behave, or you'll wait a long time."

Plumb was not buying that. "You mean, you're in no rush to settle the estate because you've already made off with the money. Hah. I told him you were not to be trusted. But would he listen?"

"Fool. He had hardly tuppence when he left. Everything had gone on his previous expeditions; only the White woman's support made the last one possible." Muster yawned. "I recall you getting a winter vacation at her expense. What did you do to earn it?"

"I won't sit here being insulted. I am going to bed." Wavering footsteps were followed by a door shutting.

Sir Ambrose groaned. "She's suing the estate for all that money back. I don't have it; you say the estate doesn't have it. What will happen to us? How will I live?"

"Your wife had some pretty jewels. Are they up the spout already?"

"She won't let me near them. Hid them somewhere as soon as we arrived. And that's not the only thing she's been cunning about. She was incognito in Venice so her father wouldn't find out she was at Carnivale, but now she says she's estranged from Main-Bearing and won't see another penny from him."

Maddie flinched. If Lord Main-Bearing heard of his supposed daughter's marriage to that wastrel, there'd be stormy weather ahead. The speedy marriage was understandable from both sides now: Sarah wanted a quick change of names and a chance at whatever the baron might bring back from his expedition, and Ambrose wanted a rich wife in a hurry, having lost his fortune at cards. A lucky escape for sweet Clarice.

Colonel Muster's voice drew her back to the recorded conversation. "And you were fool enough to marry her. Under her right name, I suppose? No getting out of it without annoying the Steamlord." There was a clink of glassware as one or the other freshened a drink. Then Muster continued. "The lawsuit against the estate can't proceed until the old lady's lawyers serve the papers. They must be served to me, since I'm the executor, until I'm declared dead. Right now nobody in London knows where I am. But there's a risk that fat detective will mention me in a report, and then the game's up."

Had Maddie mentioned Colonel Muster in the report she had just handed to Hornblower? She thought not. That one dealt with the baron's airship and his body. And, of course, the photograph showing the mask had been in the manor at some point. Did the arrogant airship magnate not realize that the impediment to her lawsuit, the vanished executor, was the same colonel who had drunk tea with her this very afternoon? Possibly not, for the quarrelsome Mrs. Midas-White might have any number of legal actions against any number of persons, and likely had teams of lawyers to handle such details for her. Should Maddie tell her? Not yet, she decided. A good investigative reporter did not reveal information merely to see ill-doers punished, but observed from the fringes while the subjects revealed even more of their secrets.

Tonight she would slip TD back into the library. Or into the parlour, if there was a chance the ladies might sit there after dinner. Perhaps leaving him in the parlour overnight would reveal whatever Lady Sarah was searching for, and save Maddie a night's lost sleep.

When the gong rang for dinner, she re-fixed the oculus and went down, hoping Lady Sarah had once again taken to her bed. She had not, but presided from the foot of the table. There was more conversation tonight, mainly from Professor Plumb and Colonel Muster, seated on either side of Mrs. Midas-White and doing their best to hold her attention. Plumb even gave up his post-prandial brandy to escort her to the ladies' parlour. Maddie and Lady Sarah followed them across the hall. There had been no sign from the latter that she recognized Maddie or paid her any notice, which was all to the good as far as Maddie was concerned. She settled herself at the small table in the parlour, not as close to the hearth as she might have liked but out of immediate notice and apt, she hoped, to be forgotten while others talked freely.

She heard nothing of value, however, merely Professor Plumb boasting. To hear him tell it, White Sky passengers had flocked to his lectures during his trans-Atlantic crossing last fall. Was he angling for an invitation to return to America on one of Mrs. Midas-White's ships? Just why did he feel the need to leave England again so soon? To escape culpability in the baron's death, or to sell a purloined Nubian mask in the vast, anonymous marketplace across the ocean? Both?

Colonel Muster soon abandoned the dining room too. He talked of petty thieves hiring onto airship crews for the easy pickings, daring jewel robberies on trans-Atlantic flights, and cardsharps preying upon young men lulled into false security by the small world of an airship. Mrs. Midas-White found nothing to query in his last assertion. If she did not know of his recent disgrace over gambling, it was another morsel of evidence that she had not acquainted herself with the details of the baron's estate. And yet she might, in any missive, mention the name to her lawyers. The colonel was taking a frightful risk by being in the same house. But then, a gambler must enjoy risks. When his oratory touched on the need for trained security forces on airship liners it was clear he was angling for a job with the White Sky Line. Such an occupation would pay him to live in the air, allowing time and distance to dim the memory of his scandalous ejection from his club.

Something crashed through the library window, bringing the parlour party to an abrupt end. While everyone else crowded to the connecting door, Maddie slipped out to the hall and hurried to the library doorway. A small, water-stained trunk lay in a spray of shattered glass and splintered casement. Surely that was the trunk from the Coast Guard Station? Sir Ambrose shoved past her into the room just as a man with a pistol in his hand clambered in through the hole.

"Where's that poltroon, Plumb?" Professor Windsor Jones, drenched and disheveled almost beyond recognition. "Plumb! Come out here and answer for your crime." Maddie tore her eyes from the weapon long enough to glance at the crowd by the other door. No Plumb. Jones charged at that door, his gun hand wavering wildly. "Where is that paltry pundit? Let me at him!"

Colonel Muster stepped forward. "You're drunk. Put that toy down and stop scaring the ladies."

"Toy?" Professor Jones stopped. "I'll show you what this toy can do." He whipped around. There was a loud pop. The painting of old Lady Bodmin above the hearth tumbled top over toes onto the floor, ending with the lady's aged head in the flames and the rest of her leaning on the grate.

"Granny!" Sir Ambrose leapt forward and dragged the portrait out of the fire, smacking at the cinders that came along. Jones made for the gap left by the upset heir, pushing past Maddie to reach the hall.

"Aha!" He bolted toward the staircase. Plumb was halfway up, huffing and holding the railing as he climbed. Jones leveled the gun. Maddie cannoned into his back, sending him staggering. The shot popped. A chunk of the newel post fell away. Jones tripped over his long coattail and fell face down, his gun flying from his hand. Maddie fell over him. Above them, Professor Plumb stumbled. Thuds and truncated wails announced his progress down the stairs.

As Maddie caught her breath, Jones coughed, sending a cloud of brandy fumes into her face. She coughed too, and scrambled away as best she could, hampered by her long, narrow skirt. Her hand came down on the pistol. She shoved it into her side pocket and kept going until her back fetched up against the newel post. Jones crawled toward her. She clutched the first thing that came to her fingers—a shattered half of the post's carved pineapple—and threw it at his face. It missed by a good margin, and he came on.

Colonel Muster planted a foot on Jones' hand. "Stop now, man, or I'll crush your fingers. You'll never pen another cockamamie conspiracy theory."

Granny!

Jones wilted.

"I think he's drunk." Maddie attempted to organize her skirt and stand up without revealing the weight of the weapon dragging her pocket down. She was only partly successful, but nobody noticed. Those now daring to venture out of the library were rushing to Professor Plumb, who had crumpled on the lowest landing.

"I perish," he groaned. "The fiend has given me a

mortal wound."

"Get up, you silly man. You fell down the stairs," Mrs. Midas-White told him. "You. Footman. Take him to the library." The morose fellow did as he was bid, hoisting the prostrate professor by an arm with no regard for possible broken bones. He plunked Plumb into an armchair, and Maddie handed back the fez that had tumbled lightly from the half-landing to the hall floor with only a stripe of dusty spider-web to show for its wild flight.

Sir Ambrose, having tenderly dusted off his Granny's face with an antimacassar, leaned her against the wall and poured out a stiff brandy. Mrs. Midas-White snatched it from his hand and pushed it at Professor Plumb.

"Drink that and pull yourself together."

Colonel Muster dragged Professor Jones into the room and flung him at the sofa. "Explain yourself, sir."

"He stole my trunk. He gave it to Baron Bodmin to find the Eye of Africa. That was my research." Jones pointed dramatically at the trunk. "It's all in there. It was with the baron when he drowned."

Maddie frowned. How had he retrieved the trunk from the coroner's boathouse? How had he known it was there at all?

Jones rambled on. "All mine. When I saw the baron came ashore with a trunk, it was mine. I knew it."

Of course, that image of the baron and the trunk had been in all the newspapers a week ago. Plenty of time for even a drunk American to find out where Cornwall was and get himself there. She hoped he had not shot anyone in stealing it back.

"Stole it, did you?" Colonel Muster abandoned his guard pose over Jones and slung the trunk up to his shoulder. "It's evidence now. I'll lock it up until the Coast Guard arrives to claim it." He strode toward the hall door, danced a short minuet with Hercule Hornblower, who had belatedly decided to investigate the commotion, and headed for the stairs. Dashing up them two at a time, he vanished from Maddie's line of sight amid the cobwebs and gloom of the upper flight.

Silence fell, thick as the settling dust. A movement near the shattered window could have been the wind touching the drapery, but it was Obie, looking in from the darkness, his eyebrows raised in a question. Maddie rolled her eyes back at him. She had not needed his help with the drunken gunman, and if she had, there would have been no time to send for him. And what were they to do with Jones? Lock him in a bedroom to sleep it off? Send for the Coast Guard to take him away?

A log popped in the hearth, startling her. She looked around. Lady Sarah stood by the parlour door, beautiful in her pallor, staring at the wreckage of the paneling above the hearth. Mrs. Midas-White sat by the fire, gazing narrow-eyed at the two professors in turn, clicking her brass claws together. Sir Ambrose poured out another brandy and guzzled it. Hornblower preened his moustaches by the hall door. Colonel Muster was doubtless searching the trunk for the Eye of Africa. He was the baron's executor, after all, and who had a better right to secure it? Except it wasn't in the trunk, as Maddie well knew. And the Coast Guard was satisfied that nobody had interfered with the contents when the trunk and body were found. If it had not gone overboard with the baron from his airship, the mask must still be in the manor. Perhaps in this very room.

She looked at Lady Sarah again. All that time spent canoodling with Baron Bodmin in Cairo; had he whispered of hiding places in his distant home, for which she was searching? Tonight TD would be charged to follow that industrious trickster around. If she found anything, Maddie wanted to know about it.

A shrill ululation split the air. Sir Ambrose dropped his glass. Lady Sarah gasped. Professor Plumb floundered upright and slid to the carpet instead. Professor Jones yawned, snorted, and turned his face to the back of the sofa. Mrs. Midas-White blew again on a silver whistle, her waxen cheeks reddening with the effort. Soon several pairs of feet came tramping down the stairs and across the hall. An officer from her airship led a contingent of crewmen into the library. The lady pointed at Jones.

"Take that man to my brig. I will speak to him in the morning, when he is sober."

"You can't do that," said Sir Ambrose. "The bounder shot up my granny. Call for the constabulary."

"He knows something about the mask. I intend to have it." Mrs. Midas-White's eyes opened full upon him, gray rimmed in black. "Unless you can pay me its value tonight." Not waiting for her hapless host's response, she told her officer, "A small White Sky trunk was taken upstairs by Colonel Muster. Find him and take the trunk to my ship."

She left the library, her spike heels rapping on the stones of the hall floor and her claws rasping on the banister as she took to the stairs. Her men slung Professor Jones bodily from the sofa and followed in a neat phalanx with him swinging insensate between them.

Hornblower shuddered. "These so-horrible people. Hercule Hornblower must bring an end before someone else is imperiled. Record all you know," he told Maddie. "Or have guessed, or suspect, about the baron's involvement with all these *crétins*." He advanced on the brandy decanter, poured the dregs into his glass, and added, "Bring it to me here. Tonight. And send the footman with another bottle, *pour aider* the grey cells."

Leaving Lady Sarah to minister to Professor Plumb, who had regained his chair amid piteous groaning, Maddie went upstairs. Professor Jones' pistol bumped against her thigh with every step. What had possessed her to take it, and keep it? Surely it would be better turned over to someone accustomed to firearms? In her chamber, she removed the weapon from her pocket and contemplated it. Then something tapped on her window.

She dropped the gun. Fortunately, it landed on the coverlet. Obie jumped into the room and snatched it as it slid toward the edge of the lumpy bed. He popped the cylinder out sideways and tilted it over his hand. A half-dozen empty cartridges tumbled out.

"That's better. You knew nothing of shooting when we last met. Where'd you pick up this pistol?"

"I still know nothing," Maddie snapped. "It's Professor Jones'. I took it after he tried to shoot Professor Plumb."

"You took it?" Obie shook his head. "Wish I'd seen that. You need a minder, girl."

"I do not! I managed quite well on my own." Her temper easing, Maddie added, "Although I would have been in difficulties if Colonel Muster had not stopped Jones coming after me."

"I dare not imagine. He'll be in Mrs. Midas-White's brig tonight, so you'll be safe enough. Remind me to teach you to shoot, though, next time we have a few days together."

"She really has a brig on a little ship like that?"

"On every ship. A law unto herself, that woman. Will she get the mask, do you think, from grilling Windy Jones?"

"Windy?"

"Short for Windsor. Or something else, if you believe Hiram about the stench in his cabin after a night of hard drinking." Obie flopped onto the bed. "Some exciting night, huh? So fill me in."

"I can't. I really must write up a report for Mr. Hornblower. He said to include everything I know, guess, or suspect. He'll take all the glory if my information leads to him solving the baron's murder." Maddie stamped her foot. "It always happens that way. I do the work and some man takes the credit."

"If you take it yourself, someone will put your picture on the aetherwire news. And if you think your father will be fooled by hair dye and an oculus, however fetching it is . . ."

"No, you're right." Maddie slumped onto a chair. "I'll write up everything, and let him have the credit. Except I'll also send articles off to CJ for the morning edition. I forgot before supper to send the one about the baron being shot rather than drowning. Now I can do one about Professor Jones bursting in too. Could you get them over to the Inn for telegraphing tonight?"

"No problem. We've got a heli-cycle aboard for messenger runs. A night flight across the moors will be cake. Unless I get lost, that is." Obie yawned. "I'll just have a nap until you're ready."

Maddie pulled out her notebook, telegraph forms, and pen. As she settled down to work, she realized TD was still sitting silent in her pocket. She pulled him out.

"I'm going to sneak down and set TD on Lady Sarah for tonight. Where's TC?"

"Left him on the library windowsill to record events there. Could be handy."

"You're a pal." Maddie slipped down the stairs again and, seeing candlelight from the little parlour, went that way. As she'd hoped, it was empty. Lady Sarah's voice came from the library, coaxing Professor Plumb to drink up and let Ambrose help him to bed. Maddie pocketed a couple of extra candles, set TD on a shelf among knickknacks, and said softly, "TD, at your discretion. Look and listen to Lady Sarah, wherever she goes, until I come back for you."

Obie was fast asleep, head askew and mouth open. Maddie lit a second candle and got down to work, writing hard and fast for CJ's morning edition, and a slower, careful summary for Hercule Hornblower, with a separate sheet as a timeline of all the suspects' known movements. After all, she knew quite a lot about these *crétins*, first from Egypt, then from the Kettle papers, and now from her own observations. How much of it would come as a surprise to the great detective? Had he an inkling at all that Lady Sarah, the new bride, was the same woman who had run off with the jewels the baron had ordered "on approval" in Cairo? Who did he think had the means, the motive, and the opportunity to kill the baron?

While she wrote for him, she pondered for herself. The mask could not have been found with the baron, or the guilty party would not remain at Bodmin Manor. Was it Lady Sarah? Could a lady so dainty manipulate the baron's body out of his airship, and abandon ship with sufficient skill as to be unscathed? Where was her husband during that episode? It was impossible to see the hapless Sir Ambrose as a co-conspirator. He was too guileless by half to keep such a secret. And was Lady Sarah sufficiently ruthless? She had not been known to kill before. That did not mean she had not, merely that she'd not been found out.

Mrs. Midas-White? Definitely ruthless. If she had the mask, though, she'd be long gone back to America, paying no further heed to the baron or his paltry estate. And she would not be so quick to snatch the drunken Professor Jones.

So much for the women in the case. Now for the men:

Sir Ambrose: too foolish to act alone. If he'd snuck off from Paris to kill the baron, he would have made a mull of the body's disposal. Unless he'd fired the fatal shot and his very clever wife had orchestrated the rest, to cover up the crime. Could Ambrose keep from babbling such doings to the other men when he was, as so often, deep in drink?

Professor Plumb might have wanted the mask for himself, but it was difficult to picture the indolent academic undertaking the effort to dispose of the body and the trunk—which was, to be sure, evidence that could discredit him with his peers by proving Jones' accusations. As for leaping from an airship over either water or land . . . the mind boggled.

Professor Jones. If he'd caught up to Baron Bodmin and found the trunk, he might have killed with a single shot. But he would never have thrown his precious research overboard. If he hadn't seen the trunk, he had no motive for the killing. Except to take the mask, if by some strange chance he'd heard about it immediately on the baron's brief return to England. If he'd seen the mask, he would have taken it, and likely fled to America by the first ship, not hung around getting into drunken rages over his lost work. And he would have taken his research with him.

Who did that leave? Colonel Muster. Again, sufficiently ruthless. As a military man, he could shoot, unless whatever kept him in dark lenses had damaged his eyesight. He had experience in airships, and she had seen him with her own eyes plummeting from the sky under a frail canopy. He needed money. But did he gain anything by the baron's death? Not obviously, not unless he happened upon the mask. Which he had not found or why seize the water-stained trunk? He had known enough, however, to chance looking for the prize there.

Frustrated by the mass of possibilities, Maddie put the final period to her report with such emphasis that the nib went through the page. Using greater care, she coded her telegrams for CJ and shook Obie awake.

"Off you go for your midnight heli-cycle tour of the moors, dear fellow."

Obie sat up, stretching. "May I look?"

She handed him the timeline. "Do you see anything amiss with this?"

He yawned and angled the page to catch the light. "In December, all your suspects were in Cairo except Ambrose, who was presumably in London making eyes at little Clarice?" She nodded. "After Christmas, the baron flew off to the desert, and Plumb and Muster returned to England. Seems straight enough. Lady Sarah—ah, that's interesting; she stayed in Cairo under a different name for a whole month, communicating with Mrs. Midas-White. Arguing over the next steps or . . .?"

"Or hatching a new scheme for when the baron returned," said Maddie. "Nobody knew then that he would not be coming back."

"A fair point. For whatever reason, she flies off to Venice using your name, drops it soon after arrival, then picks it up in mid-March, when she boards the airship with Sir Ambrose and gets married en route to Paris. As you." He grinned as Maddie let out a vexed huff. "I should hope you have better taste. They could have gone off to murder his uncle from there, if he let them know he was passing over."

"Except he brought the mask to Cornwall," said Maddie. "Why go all the way back to Paris? To meet the new bride?"

"Surprise for him if he did, given their previous association. I suspect even idle Ambrose would not remain married to his uncle's mistress. Or not without a lot of money in her future. Now to mid-

April, when the airship was found adrift. The colonel was either in London or not when it was found, and the baron is deemed to have gone into the sea between then and the sighting two weeks earlier over the Suez Canal. No more definite time than that?"

"The coroner could not be sure how long he was in the water, due to those schools of Shad picking the bones." She shuddered. "For the crucial two weeks, we have no independent accounting for the colonel's or either professor's whereabouts. Or Mrs. Midas-White's, come to that."

"Madame's minions can be on the job by morning. I'll send her a message." He folded the telegraph forms, tucked them into his jacket, and scrambled out the window. She latched the casement after him and hurried down to submit her report.

Hercule Hornblower had remained in the library with the other men. Maddie loitered in the hall before going in, unabashedly listening. Sir Ambrose whined about his wife's lack of money and attention. Colonel Muster interjected cutting comments. Hornblower recounted yet another incident in his fabulous series of detecting triumphs. All as usual. She walked into the room, presented the papers tidily clipped in order, and retreated, only to slip into the parlour from the hall entrance.

TD was still there, peering from behind a standing picture frame. She asked him to speak but nothing came out. Since it was unlikely anyone here—save perhaps Obie—had any idea how to reset his mechanism, she had to assume Lady Sarah had not yet returned to this room. After a moment to wonder if Obie had called TC away from the library windowsill as he flew away, she moved TD to the mantle. It was close to the library door. If Lady Sarah went to search the library tonight, he could listen, and maybe get into a position to see what occurred.

Chapter Sixteen

THE NIGHT WAS uneventful. On her way down to breakfast, Maddie found TD where she had left him, although turned slightly into the parlour and covered with more dust than she might have expected from a single night here. Fresh dust had been sifted onto the mantle too. The housekeeper had surely wiped it when turning out the room just yesterday. Odd. Maybe all the heavy men running up and down the stairs last night had shifted something in the ceiling. She peered upward, but the morning light from the hall was insufficient to show anything untoward amid the cobwebs. The young girl above the fireplace peered down sweetly with her painted eyes. Whatever fell on the mantle had not dimmed her new-dusted surface. Curious.

Footsteps passed in the hall as she was about to command TD to speak. Then the breakfast gong sounded and she hurried out, leaving him where he now blended in so well. There was still a chance Lady

Sarah would return to that parlour after breakfast and say or do something incriminating.

At the table, Hornblower announced, "I, Hercule Hornblower, am ready to reveal all about the mysterious death of the baron of Bodmin Manor. You will all gather in the library immediately after breakfast or expose your own guilt. Footman," he bellowed as that surly fellow came in with a fresh pot of steaming cocoa, "take a message to Madame Midas-White. She must bring her prisoner to the library in thirty minutes if she desires answers."

Nobody ate much breakfast. Maddie, picking at her kedgeree and bacon, saw preoccupation on some faces, anxiety elsewhere, a lowered brow there, and of course the bruises on Professor Plumb's face from his tumble down the stairs. But nothing she could definitively say was guilt. At the conclusion of the allotted time, they all followed the great detective into the library. She settled closest to the hall door and opened her notebook, looking unobtrusively for Obie's little sparrow on the windowsill. He was not to be seen. What recording was done would be TD's alone, from his station inside the parlour door. It was far from ideal.

Lady Sarah sat far off by the parlour door. Her husband paced before the fire. Colonel Muster took the desk chair. When Mrs. Midas-White entered, she chose the sofa facing the grate, beside Professor Plumb, while Professor Windy Jones, escorted by two burly crewmen, slouched between the two tall windows. One of these people had almost surely killed Baron Bodmin, but Maddie still was not sure which. Hercule Hornblower set himself in the corner by the hearth, effectively displacing Sir Ambrose.

The latter leaned against a bookshelf near the colonel and crossed his arms uneasily over his scrawny chest.

"Good people," said Hornblower grandly, "some of you were friends of the dead man, others his relations. One was his enemy implacable, and this person, I say to you, is in this room today." He went on in this vein for some minutes, his hands dancing for emphasis, without mentioning a single relevant detail. Maddie wondered if he'd read her notes, or fallen asleep. For that matter, would he fall asleep in the midst of his exposition?

As Maddie watched her employer, something beyond his head caught her eye. The picture of Sir Ambrose's granny, with the morning sun full upon it, was propped on the mantle, its shot-split wire coiled at its side. Above it, a neat hole could now be seen in the dark paneling. Ah, that was the source of the dust in the parlour. The bullet from Professor Jones' gun had passed through that wire last evening, straight into the paneling and out to the parlour, bringing mortar dust and wood splinters with it. Surely that was what had coated TD where he sat. Or had she moved him to that spot after the shooting? She replayed the events of the evening but could not be certain.

"To continue," Hornblower announced. One of his plump hands dropped to his waistcoat. The other pointed directly at his employer.

"Madame Midas-White," he roared at her. "Did you or did you not know the research that guided Baron Bodmin on his travels was in fact stolen? Did you kill the baron to gain that treasure? Or, when he refused to either give you the mask or repay your money, did you shoot him of your vengeance?"

Mrs. Midas-White glared at him, her brass claws clicking. "In England, I can sue you for making such an accusation."

"Hercule Hornblower accused nobody, merely asked the question: Did you kill Baron Bodmin?"

"I'd have made a better job of it. Get on, man. Who is the killer? Who stole my mask?"

Hornblower's chubby digit moved on. "Professor Plumb. You stole the research into the Eye of Africa mask from Professor Windy Jones, is it not so? Did you come to Bodmin Manor, not to catalogue the library for your friend's estate, but to claim your share of the treasure? Did you kill him when he refused to split the proceeds? Or did he threaten to reveal your theft and see you ejected from your university? Did you kill the Baron Bodmin?"

"Me? But . . . no!" Plumb sat up, miraculously forgetting all his injuries. "It was still term time when his airship appeared. Anyway, Bodmin would have told me the story of his adventures. Me, recorded for all the newssheets with the Eye of Africa in my hands? My fortune as a traveling lecturer would have been assured." Plumb sank back on the sofa, groaning from pain or the shattered dream of glory.

The pointing finger moved on. "Colonel Cardsharp, er, Muster. You were the oldest friend and the trustee of Baron Bodmin, and you had fled London several days before his airship was found adrift. Did you, being desperately short of money and about to be cast out of your regiment, kill your old friend for the treasure he may have brought back from Africa?"

Colonel Muster said nothing. The dark lenses

gave away nothing. After staring at him for a moment, Hornblower waved a pudgy hand at the distant windows.

"Professor Windsor Jones. You lost your research, the product of many years' labour. You were laughed out of Oxford. You were betrayed by a comrade in academe and beaten to the treasure and the undoubted fame that would rightfully have been yours. Did you come here to confront the baron and kill him in a fit of your undoubted American temper?"

Jones leaped forward, cursing incoherently, and the two crewmen grabbed his arms. As he struggled, Maddie could just make out Obie beyond the window, half-concealed in the ivy. When he caught Maddie's gaze, he pointed emphatically upward, mouthing something. She shrugged confusion. He pulled TC out of his jacket pocket and made a sign like a question mark in the air. Maddie pointed to the parlour, where TD remained on his lonely vigil. Obie grimaced, poked a finger at the parlour and then repeated the emphatic "up". He vanished. The ivy shook. He was climbing it, but to what purpose? Did he want her to retrieve TD and send him to the roof?

With Jones subdued, Hornblower faced Sir Ambrose. "You, sir. Perennial financial distress is your lot. You gambled away your own fortune to Colonel Muster—and nobody would blame you for wanting to murder him, if you had done so. Your hope of marrying another fortune was dashed by a woman's guile. Did you kill your uncle to inherit his estate and his new African treasure?"

The heir flattened against the bookcase. "You can't say that. Sarah, tell them we weren't here then.

It's not true!"

"Yes, we come to Lady Peacock," said Hornblower, smoothing his moustaches with both index fingers as he gazed out over his audience. "That loveliest of liars. She tried to induce the baron to take her with him on his treasure hunt. When that failed, she lured his feckless heir into marrying her instead, that she might come to the treasure by another route. Did she sneak away to Bodmin Manor to silence the baron before he could reveal to his nephew her true nature?"

At that he spun, and the attention of the room whirled with him. "What do you say, Lady Peacock?"

The chair by the parlour door was empty.

Chapter Seventeen

"LADY PEACOCK? WHERE is that woman?"

"Sarah!" wailed Sir Ambrose.

"She's the killer," yelled Colonel Muster. "I knew she couldn't be trusted." He rushed to the parlour door. Maddie slipped out to the hall. The devious widow/wife/imposter had escaped while the struggle with Windy Jones distracted everyone. That must have been what Obie had tried to tell her. But how?

Obie had been pointing upward. Maddie ran up the main stairs, along the gallery to the attic stairs and thus to the roof stair. As she burst into the bright Cornish morning, a shadow passed overhead. The White Sky airship was coming in to moor. Where had it been? And what was that rapidly vanishing blob on the horizon? She put her hand up to shield her eyes.

A small airship shimmered briefly in the full morning sunlight. Then it activated reflectors and vanished against the sky. Dangling beneath it from a rope ladder was a slender man's form. Was that Obie?

A tiny brown sparrow zoomed toward the roof and circled Maddie's head twice. With no TD to comprehend his excited twitters, he soon soared away in the direction of the cloaked ship.

Yes, it was Obie hanging off that ladder. Not for a moment did Maddie question whether he might be absconding with the Eye of Africa. No, he had followed the escaping Lady Sarah in the only way that presented itself. Doubtless he would send a message when he could. She could only hope he would get aboard the ship, and not be thrown to his death by the desperate imposter.

She was still standing, watching the general direction the ship had gone, when Mrs. Midas-White appeared on the roof. Behind her came Hercule Hornblower, moving faster than Maddie had ever seen him.

"Madame! You have not paid me yet. I demand recompense."

"Fool." The airship magnate turned on one spiky heel and stabbed her claws in his direction. "I see no murderer and no mask. Count yourself fortunate if I do not sue you for the advanced expenses back." She whirled away and stalked across the roof, ignoring Maddie. The White Sky airship unfolded its gangplank to meet her. As soon as she was on board, the ship lifted off and turned its head toward London, leaving Hornblower still yelling about his fee.

When the craft was almost out of sight, he said, "Hercule Hornblower will never work again for an

American. Pack your bag, young lady. And bespeak whatever conveyance can be found to return us immediately to that forsaken inn."

Maddie ran down to the hall, gave the footman the message about a cart, and darted between the parlour curtains to retrieve TD. He was just where she'd left him, with even more dust silted down upon his little brass head. Above him, the portrait of the smiling girl was askew. She poked the frame. It swung easily, releasing another cloud of ancient grit into her face. She blinked hard and soon saw the portrait had concealed a small wall safe. Its door was not quite shut.

Grabbing the nearest ottoman, she climbed up and pulled. The safe was empty, but its dusty floor showed where something had been. A thing about as large around as a human face, or a life-sized African mask.

Lady Sarah must have figured out the mask's location overnight and taken the opportunity of Jones' outburst to steal away with it. She must have planned to leave today in any event, for she had gone to the expense of hiring a reflector-equipped runabout to lift her from the roof. If Obie hadn't grabbed onto the boarding ladder, she'd have got clean away. And might still do so.

Maddie sagged. All the observing and puzzling and recording and reporting, and she had nothing to show for her pains. Lady Sarah, who was at the very least a thief and an imposter, was gone. Mrs. Midas-White was gone, to pursue her lawsuits and pinch her pennies. Obie was gone. Soon Maddie too would be gone, with no murderer and no mask to report to CJ. Three nights in this spider-infested pile of rocky damp, and she was ignominiously en route to London, facing joblessness yet again. What a week!

Chapter Eighteen

ON THE JOLTING ride back across Bodmin Moor, Hornblower was too enraged by his lack of payment to doze off. His grumbling monologue did nothing to ease her fury at Lady Sarah's escape. Blossoms on the hedgerows moved her not, nor did gamboling lambs. The cloudless sky mocked her. Lady Sarah the Vile Imposter was up there in her reflective, all-but-invisible airship, fleeing with whatever remained of Maddie's visiting cards, the Nefertiti jewels, and now, presumably, the Eye of Africa mask with its fabulous red-veined diamond. What had Madame Taxus-Hemlock said: that she hadn't killed but rarely left a place without a profit? Had she this time crossed her own line, killing Baron Bodmin to lift that profit to the stratosphere?

After fuming halfway to Jamaica Inn, Maddie realized she had power to foil Sarah, at least in England. She could submit an article, with TD's image from Cairo, telling of the mysterious woman fleeing England with the Eye of Africa. Every policeman, watchman, and ticket-taker in every port and terminal would be watching for Sarah. Maddie spent the last few rocky miles composing the telegraph she would send from the inn. The news could be on the streets of London before Sarah reached the metropolis. Take that, Lady Sarah!

If, indeed, London was her destination. Although Maddie had tucked TD up onto her hat, to readily receive his twin if TC found them, there was no message from Obie. How far could he fly clinging to the ladder under that little craft? Had he been hauled aboard or set down on some desolate tor? Or, worse yet, cut loose to plummet? Was he lying up there on the trackless moor, broken and bleeding?

No. All the clockwork birds were equipped with a distress program in the event their person met with an accident. Madame's family hawks flew routes between all the main English and European cities, and would immediately divert for a distress call from one of their own flock. Obie was fine. He had been in many scrapes before and come through unscathed. This time would be no different.

The cart rattled onto the cobbles by the inn as the east-bound airship approached. Clutching her hat with one hand and her portmanteau with the other, Maddie hurried inside, calling for the landlord and a telegraph form. With the telegram handed in, she counted out coins to cover it and the cost of the cut-down image of Sarah. Image transmission could take half an hour to dot-dash for every tiny square, and that was if the little puncher-bugs were working up to listed speed. She could not stay to confirm its dispatch, for the call went out to report to the roof for boarding.

As she turned away, however, the framed telegraph form on the wall caught her eye. The recipient of that telegram might have been the first, the only individual to learn of the baron's successful quest and his return to Bodmin Manor. She had intended to send a query to Madame about tracing it. When writing up Hercule Hornblower's report last night, had she told him about it? With resources she did not possess, either of them might still trace the telegram's delivery. She hurried up the narrow stairs to the rooftop gangplank, and across to the bobbing ship without a thought for the narrow gangplank or the cobblestone paving far below. Shoving rather rudely past a fat farmer's wife hung about with links of heavily garlicked sausages, she flung herself into a seat across from her employer to gasp out the information.

"Should I care now?" Hornblower shrugged beneath his shoulder cape and tugged the astrakhan collar tighter around his throat. "I am dismissed, like an incompetent footman. Hercule Hornblower is no lackey to be flung out on a whim. What care I now for some telegram the baron sent? It will earn me no money and no fame, and I will expend not one molecule of my invaluable grey cells upon it. Speak to me no more."

"Does that mean I'm fired, too? No more report-writing when we get back to London?"

"I have no further need of your service. You, however, will be paid for your days here. Hercule Hornblower does not Welshman upon his workers like Americans do."

Well, so much for that job. Maddie would hide herself with Madame and see if Lady Serephene had made her a new evening gown or forgotten all about it. Another job would come, somehow, somewhere. Maddie had acted the parlourmaid when she first ran away; she could do it again. Even on a White Sky airship if need be. Back to boring brown hair, though. Purple was too noticeable for a parlourmaid. She rested her elbow on the chair-arm and her chin on her hand, staring out the window as the moors receded beneath the keel.

There was no news from Obie at Exeter either. After a quick lunch Maddie was London-bound, and she had nothing to do but worry about Obie in the intervals of wondering how to trace one telegraph from weeks ago among all the thousands that came to London daily. She accepted Hornblower's pay in the Central London terminal and, while his imposing figure parted the crowds en route to the taxi rank, she slid away, one working woman among hundreds, to the self-propelling streetcar.

"Claridge's Hotel," she answered the girl sharing her seat as the streetcar lurched forward. "I'm visiting an old employer there. And you?"

She had hardly tapped on the corner suite's door before Madame pulled her into the room with an exclamation.

"Thank heavens you didn't dawdle. We have only an hour to get you refitted for your next assignment."

Chapter Nineteen

THE LUXURIOUS STATEROOM was deserted, its lady occupant singing in her bath while Maddie stacked up the breakfast things. A *London Fog & Cog* lay open on the table, one corner soaking up butter and jam. Maddie flipped rapidly through the greasy newsprint and was rewarded by the sight of Imposter Sarah's face, slightly enlarged and grainy, under a 15-point headline asking "Have You Seen This Woman?"

Investigating the last days of Baron Bodmin, this paper has learned he was keeping company with a lovely young widow whose name proved fictional. This woman, pictured above, was seen weeping at the aerodrome as Bodmin departed on his ill-fated treasure hunt. She stealthily departed Cairo under another assumed name, carrying away a small fortune in Egyptian jewelry set with diamonds, rubies, and lapis lazuli, all obtained through devious means. Posing as the wife of Bodmin's heir, Sir Ambrose Peacock, this imposter arrived in England in March.

Yesterday this same woman fled Bodmin Manor, Cornwall, carrying away the Eye of Africa mask, which the baron had hidden in his home before his mysterious death. It is not known at this time if she was involved in his demise, but inquiries are being made. She is presumed to be attempting to flee the country.

If you see this woman, do not approach her but alert the nearest law officer. If you know this woman by any name, please inform the Fog's nearest office and we will ensure the information reaches the proper authorities.

Not that the article would avail now, if Obie's information was correct. Maddie collected the tray and let herself out of the First Class (with balcony) parlour stateroom. Along the corridor, Obie, in his white steward's uniform, was raising his hand to tap at a door. She nudged him in passing and dodged into the first service pantry, sure he would follow.

Crowding behind her into the narrow galley between cupboards and dumb-waiter, he asked, "Did you spot her?"

"No. I've been in every First Class cabin now, too. Are you one hundred percent sure she embarked on this airship?"

"I watched her with my own eyes. She'd changed clothes on the passage from Cornwall, to something brown and boring, but it was her right enough. There wasn't another woman on that little courier airship.

I could see most of it from the cargo compartment."

"I'm so glad you didn't travel all that way to London dangling from a ladder," said Maddie. "But for her to embark on a transatlantic crossing under the very nose of Mrs. Midas-White! It's insanity. Not that the owner brushes elbows with the traveling hoi-polloi. She wouldn't even allow Hornblower to travel to Cornwall with her. The other maids say she rarely leaves her cabin except for tours of inspection."

"This ship's the kind of risk a confidence woman would take." Obie off-loaded the dirty dishes from her tray into the appropriate bins. "One place nobody would expect the lovely Sarah to be. But if she's not in First Class, she must be in Second. Dozens of women up there, all bunking in random pairs. I was too slow off the mark to get her current name from the boarding steward; she'd waited until a gaggle of women came along and mingled with them. Half of them were wearing brown suits too."

"Working women do. They don't show the dirt." Maddie gave her tray a wipe and stacked it with the others. "On to Second Class then. What if we don't find her?"

Obie flicked her cheek with a finger. "We will. We've another forty hours to New York yet. Don't forget to look out the windows first thing tomorrow morning. You might catch a glimpse of Greenland."

"We've been there, Obie. Did you forget stealing that dogsled?"

"It stole me. All twenty-four legs running like stink as soon as I fell into the seat. You're finding your way around the ship all right?"

"It's identical to the one we flew on from Cairo to

Venice. I thought trans-oceanic ones would be bigger."

Obie shrugged. "Cheaper to make them all the same, I expect. Anyway, Professor Jones is at ship's liberty, bunking in Second Class 13. It's an inside single cabin. He'd likely not recognize you anyway, seeing as he was tanked to the goggles at Bodmin Manor. And Professor Plumb's in Second 22, on the other corridor. I'd like to know how he wangled another guest-lecturer passage."

"He was making eyes at Mrs. Midas-White at the Manor. I suppose this is what he was after. But why does he want to go back to America already? And on the same ship as Professor Jones, too."

"I hope they don't run into each other." Obie stuck his head out into the corridor. "All clear. Next lull when they all go down for supper. Meet me outside the staff mess-hall at seven to compare notes."

Maddie climbed up the nearest steep stairs to the Second Class corridor. She cranked up a towel-cart as she'd been shown, imprinted it with her ID tag, and it followed her obediently as she began working her way along the staterooms. If Lady Sarah was up here, the Eye of Africa mask was too, for TD had faithfully recorded her search of the paneling above the fireplace in the Bodmin Manor parlour. Although his oculii weren't entirely adapted for dim lighting, they had easily picked up the gleam of a very large gemstone in the midst of a dark blob approximately the size of a human face. Would Sarah dare to keep the mask in a shared stateroom? Would she dare leave it anywhere out of her sight?

At each door, Maddie tapped, called out, and then

opened. No waiting, not for Second Class. Twice she surprised people in states of undress, handed in their towels, and retreated before they could demand her name to complain. If they did make a fuss, well, she intended leaving the ship in America anyway, traveling with Obie and sending home articles to CJ as long as he'd pay for them. Assuming they could wrap up the Eye of Africa affair first, while they had the erstwhile Lady Sarah trapped on board. She rapped, flung open another door, and gasped.

Colonel Muster's dark lenses looked up from a schematic-covered desk that was crowded in beside the stateroom's sole bed. "What?"

"Towels, sir," she said, in a wobbly approximation of an American accent. What was he doing here?

He pointed to a rack by the tiny closet and bent over his papers. She exchanged the towels while keeping her face turned away, and crept out without drawing his further attention. Her hands shook as she stuffed the used linens into the bin on the cart and walked on. He had not seemed to recognize her, either as the brown-haired journalist from Cairo or the purple-tressed secretary from Cornwall, but who knew how much he truly saw from behind those lenses?

"Maggie," she reminded herself fiercely. "My name now is Maggie Hatley from Portsmouth, New Hampshire."

When she reported to the crew mess-hall for early lunch, there he was again, at the head of the room with the Chief Steward. His expression was unreadable. Had he fingered her after all?

"Staff, attend," the latter barked. "Our new head of fleet security will address you while you eat."

Muster took a pace forward, his military bearing ominous among the less restrictive hierarchy of the civilian airship liner. He turned his face from one side of the narrow room to the other. When satisfied he had all their attention, he spoke, coldly and to the point.

"I will be reviewing all personnel records and conducting spot inspections of all duty stations during the remainder of this voyage. Answer my questions promptly and truthfully, and you won't have a problem. Anyone caught pilfering or lying will be brigged in transit and turned over to shore authorities at our destination. That is all."

He strode out. By the uneasy glances around her, Maddie thought she might not be the only person whose file was not entirely truthful. Would she first see America from the brig? No, she would simply dodge Muster whenever she saw him. It was only thirty-seven hours now. She could manage.

But when she next saw the colonel, he had no interest in interviewing her. On the port-side Promenade, in the continual breeze of the airship's forward movement, he was overseeing the slinging-down of one of the liner's small messenger craft from its pod up in the envelope. Somewhat larger than a pterodactyl in the British Museum, the machine had similar wings and a skin of stretched, oiled canvas. When it was level with the railing, crewmen cranked up the machine's central gear and hoisted the contraption over the side. Muster clambered out onto the frail, folded wing and strapped on a flying helmet. He raised one gloved fist in a heroic pose before hopping down into the cockpit. Crewmen swung the sling out parallel to the airship. The tail-feathers waved. The wings creaked out to full extension. Ladies and gentlemen crowded the railings to watch as the craft's wings angled to take the wind, and gasped as one when it dropped smoothly away from the airship.

"How will he ever catch up?" one young lady asked. "There's nowhere for him to land," said another. "He wouldn't do it if it weren't safe," a slim gentleman assured them.

Maddie, well remembering his heart-stopping plunge from a tethered balloon in Cairo, thought he didn't much care about danger if there was applause and adulation to be gained. She moved through the crowd with her tray of magazines, following the deck stewards with their travel blankets and extra cushions, but wasn't surprised that most passengers clustered at the railing.

Between their backs she caught glimpses of the messenger craft. First it swooped low, losing way against the airship, and then, with a slight shift in the wings and a spin of the central gear, it soared upward again, higher and faster, passing only a wingspan from the vast gas envelope. At the top of one such arc it flipped right over. Amid shrieks and gasps from the watchers, Colonel Muster's flying helmet turned toward them, upside down. Sun glinted off his dark lenses. His teeth gleamed in a maniac grin. He flipped his small craft right-side up and dropped away again, down and to the rear. This time he fell so far behind that passengers began uneasily to turn away, muttering.

The craft purred forward again, up-up-up and higher still while the viewers strained to follow that speck against the sun. It vanished, taking its whirring gear and wing-noise with it. For a long moment, the breeze along the airship's deck struts was the only sound. Then the whirring grew again, and as passengers craned their necks in wonder, the machine's long beak rose from beneath. Wings straining, central gear spinning wildly, it climbed directly upward and leveled out alongside the railing. With one more mad whirl from the gear, it slid smoothly into the sling, folded its wings and was still.

"Begorrah, did you see that?" "He looped right around the liner!" "That's airmanship, sir. By gad, that's airmanship."

Colonel Muster leapt to the deck. Adoring passengers clustered around the aeronautical daredevil. The messenger craft reversed its sling-bound journey back up to storage inside the envelope. After a while the fuss died down. Maddie's basket was eventually emptied of reading material, and she spent the next hours running back and forth to fetch items for passengers. On one such foray, she came out of a First Class parlour stateroom with a knitting basket, just as a woman in a brown walking suit stepped out of the next door along.

Lady Sarah! In First Class after all.

As Maddie stepped back into the doorway, eyes downcast to avoid notice, the next piece clicked into place. The stateroom Lady Sarah had just left belonged to Mrs. Midas-White. What was she up to? Still staring at the back of the brown suit as it paced smoothly away, Maddie started off in the other direction with the knitting.

She hadn't gone three steps before bumping into someone. She dropped the bag. Bright balls of yarn began to unroll down the sky-blue carpet, skittering hither and yon with the airship's gentle sway. She scrambled after them, and only realized who she had bumped into when Mrs. Midas-White's brass claws dug into her shoulder.

"You! Girl. What's your name?"

"H-Hatley, Ma'am. Maggie Hatley."

"You weren't watching your steps. You'll be off this ship at the next port if there's a single other demerit on your record."

"Yes, Ma'am."

Mrs. Midas-White walked back into her stateroom and shut the door, leaving Maddie on the carpet staring after her.

"Gorgon," she muttered.

Chapter Twenty

"I TELL YOU, Obie," she hissed outside the mess-hall later, "they were both in that stateroom at the same time. *Together*. There's more going on here than meets the oculus."

"Didn't Madame say the lady reported to the gorgon while in Cairo? Could they have been working together all along?"

Maddie raised a doubting eyebrow. "Would any woman marry a weed like Sir Ambrose as part of a job?"

"You're a woman; you tell me." Obie frowned, working out the permutations. "If they were after the mask together, it makes sense now."

"What does?"

"The reflective courier airship was hired from a White Sky subsidiary. I didn't think much of it at the time, because anyone can hire those ships. But Mrs. Midas-White's own cruiser was conveniently standing off when the other one swooped over the rooftop. I thought it had gone for refueling but . . ."

"If they were in it together, then she may have handed over the Eye of Africa already. That would explain why Mrs. Midas-White was suddenly eager to leave England instead of pursuing her lawsuit."

"Or," said Obie, pulling her aside as exhausted chambermaids trooped past for supper, "Lady Sarah still has it and is bargaining for a better price."

"Either way, would they kill the baron to arrive at this point, or was their charade at Bodmin Manor a reaction to his unexpected death at someone else's hands?" Maddie leaned against the wall and put her hands to her temples. "I don't see either of them staging the killing so elaborately. Pushing him down the stairs at his home would be much more convenient, and what would they care if the trunk full of Jones' research was found there? It would only throw suspicion back on Jones."

Obie's stomach rumbled ominously. "We're not solving anything standing here. Let's eat. Afterward we may be able to track the lady to her chamber. Who knows? She may give us straight answers once she sees the jig's up?"

"I doubt she knows what a straight answer is. But maybe I can coerce her into giving back my visiting cards. At least then she won't wring any more free rides out of them." Maddie lifted away from the wall, shaking out her tired shoulders. "As for the murderer, we won't know that until we learn who received Baron Bodmin's telegram. What's the earliest Madame can get a message to us without going through the ship's telegraph operator?"

"Fifteen hours. We'll be cruising south along the

North American coast by then. Hawks could find us any time from dawn onward."

Maddie was sure she'd stay awake all night, plotting what to say when she finally confronted the false Madeleine Main-Bearing, but two days on the hop around the ship had worn her out. She slept hard in the airless little dormitory allotted to crew members, and woke reluctantly when the first gong sounded throughout the crew cabins. A fresh breeze wafted along the corridor from somewhere; definitely warmer than yesterday. When she descended to a deck with windows she saw, to starboard and down a thousand feet or so, a handful of small airships puttering along above a rocky coastline. No buildings, much less cities, were visible. They must be just off Canada.

The crew members in the mess hall were paying into the pool on first sight of the Statue of Liberty, with odds strongest for teatime this afternoon. Everyone looked forward to shore leave in America's largest port. Everyone except Maddie, who could not worry about a future beyond the confrontation that must happen today.

"What if I don't manage to tackle her?" she half-whispered to Obie. "Once she's ashore, we'll lose her for good!"

He nodded. "Too many solo women this trip. I've said 'brown suit, brown hair' to every steward and waiter on board, and the unvaried answer is 'which one?'" He raised his voice. "Any of you taken meals to a woman in Second Class?" Everyone looked, but nobody answered. After a moment the hum of conversation went on just as before. "So much for that. We'll just have to keep our eyes open. I'm on duty outside the Public Rooms. If she appears near the library, dining room, lounge, or spa, I'll risk sending TC to alert you. Keep your eyes peeled in the stateroom corridors. Hover in the serving pantries when you can, to watch comings and goings."

Maddie put her hand into her pocket, checking on TD and, latterly, her notebook. With its jottings, she could work up a nice article about trans-oceanic airship travel for some magazine or other. Maybe, if she couldn't solve the murder or confront the imposter to kick-start her career in investigative journalism, there might be a future for her in travel writing.

The immediate future, however, was one of delivering breakfast trays in First Class, collecting them again, and pausing often to aid the ladies in locating misplaced fans or re-lacing a boot when their own maids were absent. She tried to school her features during these menial tasks; she too had once been accustomed to calling for service rather than doing the least thing for herself. A long time ago, it seemed now. Dodging an inspection tour by Mrs. Midas-White, which was attended by Colonel Muster and seemingly every ship's officer not immediately needed elsewhere, she hurried the last tray into the service pantry.

While she was in there, Obie stopped by. "Message from Madame. The Jamaica Inn telegraph went to a message drop at the Royal Air Arms Club in St. James Street, London. Colonel Muster was a member until his recent disgrace, and Windy Jones had visitors' privileges due to some youthful service scouting in Mexico. She's looking into which of them might have been in residence then. They're both on this ship and at least one of them is armed. You need to steer clear until we figure this out."

"I'm more interested in Sarah than in them. Since she's not a killer, I'm safe confronting her."

"You don't know how far she'll go if she's cornered. Send for me if you need help." Obie touched her cheek with one finger. "Yes, I know you're a modern, independent woman. I just want you to be safe." Maddie smiled at him and slipped out the door. Satisfied that Lady Sarah was not anywhere in that section, she moved to the next deck up.

She had barely set foot on the runner-covered catwalk that served as the Second-Class hallway floor when she saw a brown-haired, brown-suited woman stepping carefully down into the next stairwell. She whirled on the spot. Grabbing the steep railings with both hands, she swung herself down five steps and another five to the level she had just left. A moment's straightening of her sky-blue uniform and starched white cap, and she was stepping out of the First Class stairwell just as her quarry passed.

Back straight, skirts swaying gently, Lady Sarah trod the hall toward the bow. At Mrs. Midas-White's door she stopped. After tapping and waiting while Maddie passed her to enter the next serving pantry, she did something at the handle and stepped inside the stateroom. The door closed.

Maddie pulled TD from her pocket. "Listen," she commanded. "Obie, she's in the gorgon's stateroom. Where is the gorgon?"

She added an injunction to TD to stay near the ceilings and escape through an outside window rather than risk capture. The little bird skimmed the gilt-touched ceiling mouldings toward the stern, leaving her to gather up a stack of fresh, white table linens. She carried this across the corridor, gave a perfunctory tap at Mrs. Midas-White's door and walked in.

Chapter Twenty-One

LADY SARAH WAS not in the parlour. Bedchamber and balcony doors stood open. A breeze from outside stirred the draperies and fluttered the plumes that stood in a brass urn beside them. Maddie put the stack of tablecloths and napkins on the dining table and, thankful for thick carpeting that muffled her footsteps, stepped up to the open bedchamber door, where a faint tapping originated.

The nefarious imposter was once again searching for hidden panels. This time she stood on the vast bed with its signature sky-blue coverlet and clouds of white pillows. As Maddie drew breath to announce herself, a section of walnut veneer slid aside under Sarah's hand. Inside was a small wall safe, to which the schemer applied a brass box. She fixed an armature to the safe's dial. A whirr, a lilac glow, and an audible clunk signaled the lock had been breached. One dainty white hand detached the box while the other opened the safe door. On the top shelf lay a velvet bag, and a leather coin sack, and a double stack of banknotes. Underneath were jewel cases and a sheaf of papers.

Sarah ignored everything but the bag. She tugged the drawstring and pulled out a dark object, as thick as two hands pressed palm to palm and as large around as a human face. It was polished ebony, set with white shells, and streaked with dried brownish stains. A gem on its forehead sparkled in the light from the balcony.

The Eye of Africa.

The imposter was caught in the very act of stealing the legendary mask. What was that legend about evildoers' blood? It did not glow red when she touched it, but then, even if the legend were true, Sarah's blood was safe within her skin. Evil as she undoubtedly was, the mask did not need to denounce her. Maddie would be more than happy to ensure she did not escape this time.

"I'll be summoning Security, madam."

Sarah turned so fast her shoe snagged on a pillow. Flailing for balance, she took in Maddie's sky-blue uniform and relaxed.

"No need, girl. I am retrieving this for the owner."

"I doubt that." Maddie stepped further into the room and shut the door behind her. "She didn't give you the combination."

"There's lots of money in here too. How much would it take for you to go away and forget you saw me?" Sarah eased off the bed and stood, shaking out her skirts with one hand. The diamond winked in the other. If it had red in its heart, Maddie could not tell. But what other diamond could be of such size, in such a mask?

"You have something I want more than money."

"You can't have this mask." Sarah stepped away from the bed. Would she make a break for the balcony?

"Yet you must have given it to Mrs. Midas-White," said Maddie, feeling behind her for the door latch, wishing she had not been in such haste to shut the woman in. "In exchange for passage to America, by any chance?"

"She promised to pay me for months of work. Now she's reneging." Lady Sarah darted out the balcony door. Maddie wrenched open the door behind her, leaped out, and caught the thief by the arm as the woman raced through the parlour. She swung Sarah around and yanked the mask from her hand.

As she backed away, Sarah grabbed at it. "Give it back. I earned it."

"I don't care about the mask," said Maddie, and was surprised to find it true. Now that she had the imposter in her sights, all her mind was bent on one object: to prevent her ever using the Main-Bearing identity again. "I want the visiting cards you stole from me in Cairo, and your promise never to use that identity again."

"Cairo?" Sarah lowered her arms and regarded Maddie with her head a-tilt. "Which cards exactly? I acquired a few."

"They were in my inkwell." Maddie sidled, putting an armchair between her and the thief. "In my chamber, down the corridor from yours."

"Inkwell." Sarah's eyes flickered while she thought. "Oh, yes. A steamlord's daughter. Useful identity, that. I don't see why we can't share it." She

195

too shifted position.

"I will not share it."

"The trail would be more confused if we were using it at the same time on different continents." Sarah sounded eminently reasonable.

"That is my identity." Maddie's voice slipped into the autocratic tone of one who has largely been obeyed since birth.

Sarah's eyes widened. "Oh my gears and goggles! *You* are the Honourable Madeleine Main-Bearing?"

Maddie bit her lip. She had not intended to give that much away.

"But why? Working at menial jobs instead of living in luxury beyond imagining?" Curiosity did not stop Sarah circling partway around the chair. Maddie shifted too, until she was almost back to the bedroom door. To her left, the curtains by the balcony wavered. Was it the wind, or had Obie arrived to help her capture Sarah?"

"That luxury is a gilded cage," she said, by way of distracting the woman. "You couldn't have stood being married to Sir Ambrose another day. Imagine being shackled to someone like that for life, because your family arranged it."

"You were escaping an arranged marriage? Supporting yourself?" Sarah edged closer. "That's very brave."

"You nearly ruined it all for me by using my identity. If my father learned of it, he'd have me shipped to a convent in the Shetland Isles."

"The Shetlands . . . is that quite far north in Scotland?"

"Yes. A horrid, desolate, windswept stack of rocks in a churning, storm-wracked sea. Supporting myself is better by far. Although I'm not living in the luxury you do. Those jewels you took from Cairo were worth far more than my pittance as a fashion reporter."

"Mrs. Midas-White refused to pay me for half a year's work, because I lost the baron before he found the mask. Those jewels are merely recovering my expenses."

"That's between you and Mrs. Midas-White," said Maddie. "I can write the story either way. Now, where are my visiting cards?"

"In my cabin. We can walk up together." Lady Sarah glanced around the parlour. "It's not safe to linger here anyway. I'll just shut the safe and make all smooth." She took two steps forward. Maddie took two steps sideways. Sarah looked past Maddie and gasped as a shadow fell into the room.

"It took you long enough, Obie," said Maddie, just before she was struck hard between the shoulder blades.

She sprawled over the carpet, ending in a heap against an armchair. The mask fell half underneath it. Shoving it further under to be out of immediate danger, she rolled onto her back.

Colonel Muster was advancing on Sarah. "Where is it?"

Sarah said nothing, sliding along the paneling toward the open bedroom door. Muster's left hand swung at her corset, knocking her sideways. She crashed against the table, tipping a vase of hothouse blossoms, and leaned there, gasping for breath. Across the room, Maddie scrambled to get her feet under her without tangling in her skirts.

Muster stepped up to Sarah again. "I know you've

got it. The safe is open. Give it to me and maybe I won't throw you overboard." He raised his right hand.

Maddie leapt. Wrapping both hands around his wrist, she dug her heels into the carpet and clung. He flung her backward in a single, effortless wave of his arm. She tripped over the armchair and lay across it, dazed.

Muster had followed her. His fingers grazed her throat. "Where's the mask, girl?"

Sarah backed into the bedroom. She must be giving up on the mask, going for the money in the safe. That tiny bit of outrage was the last attention Maddie could spare as the colonel's thumb pressed on her windpipe. She choked. He put a second hand on her throat, pulling her upright. His teeth gleamed. He repeated his question.

Maddie clawed at his hands, shredding the skin, desperate to breathe. She'd give him the mask sooner than her life. But she could not get the words past his squeezing fingers. Spots whirled in her eyes.

With a resounding bong, the brass urn full of plumes bounced off the colonel's ear. He reared back. Dropping Maddie, he clapped his bloody hand to the side of his head. He staggered toward Sarah, who was retreating, holding up the mask's bag, leading him away.

Maddie rolled off the chair, gasping for breath. By the time she got to her knees, Muster had stalked Sarah halfway around the parlour. As he reached for the bulging velvet bag that had held the mask, blood oozed from the scrapes on his hands and wrists. Any moment now, he would grab Sarah instead of the bag. Maddie stretched to grasp the brass urn.

Ignoring the feathers that fluttered to the floor, she struggled upright again. Staggering forward, she raised the pot and swung with all her might at Muster's swollen ear. Another off-key bong and his dark glasses flew off. He slumped sideways, bleeding from a gash on his cheek. As he collapsed to the carpet, groaning, Sarah scuttled out of his reach.

"Thanks," she told Maddie. "Are you okay?"

Maddie grabbed Sarah's arm to hold herself upright. "I think so. Just dizzy. You?"

"Just terrified." Sarah led Maddie to a chair by the dining table. She pulled a linen napkin from the velvet bag, dampened it from the spilled flower water and wiped the smears of Muster's blood from Maddie's throat and fingernails. "He'd have killed either of us for that mask."

Her neck aching from the colonel's assault, Maddie nodded cautiously. "He must have killed the baron for it, maybe right on top of Bodmin Manor before moving the airship. He was one of only two people who could have been told Bodmin was back in England. He may have thought the mask was hidden on the airship. When he couldn't find it, he set it adrift to confuse the trail, and searched the manor."

Muster groaned again.

Sarah twisted the blood-streaked napkin in her hands, staring at the bright streaks of red on the carpet around the colonel's head. "Had we better tie him up? I don't dare be found here, but I can't leave you alone with him. And I don't suppose you'll let me leave with the mask, either." She looked around. "Where is it?"

Colonel Muster rolled to his feet, dragging the

mask from beneath the chair in the same movement. He staggered out to the balcony.

"He's getting away!" Maddie wavered as she stood up but went after him, with Sarah close behind.

Outside, the sun bounced off something bright. Beyond the railing, still tucked in its sling, bobbed one of the airship's messenger craft. Its wings were already extended, its central gear ticking gently over. It waited only for a pilot.

The colonel stumbled toward the railing, his bloody fingers clutching the mask. Chirps and whistles filled the air. TD and TC, metal wings churning madly, darted around the murderer's head. His blood-smeared hand flailed at them. Maddie called the birds away lest they be damaged. They zoomed through the doorway to perch on her shoulders.

"Images," she told them, determined to get proof that she, herself, had not stolen the mask.

One of Muster's feet was up on the rail. Both feet. The mask winked in his hand. A red gleam tickled the huge diamond. A trick of the light?

A beam of red shot out, angled toward the colonel's face. It grabbed his unprotected gaze. He flung his free hand over his eyes, splattering more blood. The mask blazed with unholy fury. As the watchers cringed away, Muster screamed. He dropped the mask.

Its red glare winking out, the black face floated down to land on the outstretched wing of the messenger craft. Muster scrambled after it, crawling forward on his knees. He touched it again. The light blazed up.

He reared upright in the red glare. He mouthed

something that might have been, "Help me."

As Maddie and Sarah ran forward, the mask's hellacious glow ballooned. Their limbs slowed, their breath seared. Eyes burning, they barely saw Muster stagger. He skidded over the wing and tumbled right off. His scream blew away on the breeze.

The mask, its glare winking out again, floated down after him.

Released from their temporary paralysis, the two women ran toward the railing. The mask was a black dot whisked hither and yon by the stiff sea winds, its diamond winking where the sun caught it. Beyond it, falling faster, was Colonel Muster. Beneath him was only the blue expanse of the Atlantic Ocean, overseen by a rocky shore still many miles distant. He had stopped screaming.

Maddie watched, willing him to pull a cord, make a canopy appear to save his miserable life. For all his evil deeds, he was a man, and had once been a war hero.

A trick of the light?

Chapter Twenty-Two

COLONEL MUSTER WAS so far below when he hit the water that they didn't see a splash. As Maddie clutched the railing, shaking in every limb, Sarah pulled her arm. "We've got to get out of here."

It was too late. As they stepped into the parlour, Mrs. Midas-White entered like a tornado, her skirts whirling and voice shrieking.

"Thieves. Murderers. Arrest them." Behind her filed half a dozen crewmen. They spread out across the doorway and stared at the wreckage, then at the women. Obie was among them. Maddie let go of Sarah and curtsied, simultaneously straightening her cap and smoothing her apron.

"It was Colonel Muster, Ma'am. I came in to freshen the tables and he was here, on your bed, pulling stuff out of your wall safe. He choked me and said he'd kill me. I screamed, and this lady ran in from the hall and beat him off me. Then I had to hit him with the urn when he tried to kill her. He pulled something out of the bag, a black thing, and ran out to the balcony. Oh, Ma'am. He lost his footing and fell into the sea!"

Mrs. Midas-White stared at her, narrow gray-black eyes growing wide with horror. "He fell? With my mask? Noooo . . ." She rushed to the balcony railing and stared over.

Obie hurried forward. "Young ladies, you must be very distressed. Here, let me help you to a chair. Would you like a cup of tea?"

The other crewmen took his lead, albeit with a few uneasy glances at the balcony, where their employer was waving her brass claws and uttering imprecations as she peered down. Two officers went into the bedchamber and began making an inventory of the safe's contents. Soon a tea service appeared, in the hands of a wide-eyed parlourmaid. She served the two girls, mopped up the table, and went to her knees to begin smudging up the blood from the sky-blue carpet. Mrs. Midas-White would not be happy at having to replace that carpet, Maddie thought irrelevantly, and then the lady herself returned, and the moment of calm was over.

"They are lying. They stole my mask and murdered my head of security. Search them and throw them in the brig."

Chapter Twenty-Three

IN THE NARROW passage outside Maddie's dormitory, Obie beckoned with his head. Maddie pulled Sarah along as he moved a few paces from the open door. Muffled sounds of a search could be heard within, and Maddie kept her voice barely above a whisper.

"Quick thinking, Obie. Thanks. If anyone else had taken charge, we'd be sitting in the brig now. Are there really ugly drunks in there?"

"Just Professor Jones. He was waving his gun during Plumb's lecture."

"I thought until the last possible minute that he might be the murderer."

"You forgot he's afraid of flying, didn't you? He'd never have been able to jump out of an airship."

"Murderer?" Sarah joined in. "Why would he kill Baron Bodmin? And why are you helping us?"

"Long story," said Maddie and Obie together.

Maddie went on, "After losing the mask to Sarah,

Muster came aboard this ship with Mrs. Midas-White, maybe just to escape England and maybe to steal whatever he could. I don't see how he could have known where the mask was."

"He came after me this morning," said Sarah. "He saw my picture in the aether-news. I told him I'd given it to Mrs. Midas-White already. When I crept in here, I made sure he was attending her inspection. I thought I was safe until New York." A self-deprecating laugh escaped her. "The worst mistake I made on this job was underestimating him." She glanced over her shoulder, but the designated crewmen were still searching every bunk in Maddie's dormitory. "You said someone else could have known the baron had found the mask. Who?"

"Professor Jones," said Maddie. "He was a temporary member of the same club where the baron sent a telegram on his arrival home. As well as being too afraid of airships to jump out of one, he would never have parted from his trunk full of research. But the mask was in the manor the whole time. How did you know where to look?"

"Hints from Bodmin in Cairo. His mother guarded his secrets, he said. I didn't know that old bat over the fireplace was his mother until Ambrose said. It wasn't a stretch to realize she was the girl in the parlour too."

That explained that. Maddie looked at Obie. "How do I get out of this one?"

"Once your dorm is confirmed clean, I'll have you searched and leave you there. We'll repeat the process with Miss . . . Lady . . ." He shrugged. "Sarah. Then I'll report to Mrs. Midas-White that you're both innocent of the mask's theft. Did Muster really go off the balcony?"

"Oh yes. TD and TC captured it all. But we can't use them to prove Muster was the villain."

"That we can't." Obie understood without her explaining: they could not expose Madame's lovely little birds with all their secret skills. "Unless . . . I might be able to rig something plausible about a hidden security camera ordered installed by Muster as his excuse for going to her quarters while she was out. Assuming the gorgon leaves that stateroom long enough for me to put one there."

"That's you fixed," said Sarah with sudden fierceness. "But she'll have me in chains before she's through. The jewels from Cairo are in my luggage. If she claims I stole those, who will believe me that she owes that much and more? I can't fight her in court. I don't have a Steamlord papa to make it all go away, Lady Madeleine."

Obie's eyes opened wide. "You *told* her?"

"She guessed, when I demanded my cards back."

Sarah bit her lip. "I hate to do this after you saved my life today, but since you've got a friend on board and I don't, you're both going to help me out of this mess or I'm going to tell the world where Lord Main-Bearing's missing daughter is."

"Obie?"

"Up to you," he said. "If you want me to help her, I will."

They'd barely settled on a makeshift plan when the two officers returned to the hallway. One shrugged, holding up empty hands. Obie gave Maddie a nudge toward her quarters. "You'll stay there until the inquiry is concluded. Miss. I'll make sure you're let out and no mark on your record."

He escorted her inside, and Maddie slipped TD to him. Then she opened the ventilator above the door as wide as it would go, sat down on her bunk, and waited for the little bird to come back with news.

Why had she acquiesced so readily to helping Lady Sarah escape? The woman had threatened all her freedom and financial security.

But it was only too plausible that Mrs. Midas-White refused to pay Sarah for her time because the results had not been profitable. She had refused to pay Hercule Hornblower, too. And Sarah had been ready to deal reasonably with Maddie over the false ID. And, when it came down to it, she had returned to draw Colonel Muster off Maddie when she could have cleaned out the safe and run away, leaving Maddie to be murdered. Whereas Maddie's vengeful article and image in yesterday's news had led Colonel Muster straight to Sarah, and put them both in peril of their lives. Yes, Sarah was owed some consideration. *If* she gave up those visiting cards and never mentioned Maddie's name again.

It seemed hours had passed, but it was not quite lunchtime when TD fluttered in the ventilator. "Speak," she told him.

Obie's voice said, "Retrieved your cards from Lady Sarah's stateroom. The images came out great. I'll leave one with the ship for evidence of Muster's death and keep the rest for your articles. They're bound to be sensational. The gorgon will be in the cockpit during mooring. She likes to watch the approach to any port, likely to make sure they're not wasting fuel. I'll fix a recorder above her balcony then and fly Sarah away on the messenger craft that Muster left ready. She can't carry much so can you go pack up the rest of her gear and bring it off with yours once the ship is moored? Hiram's cousin will come to let you out soon. Once you're in port, he'll bring you safe to a rooming house run by his aunt, and then we can worry about our next jobs. Because I doubt the White Sky Line will take either of us back. See you in the Big Apple, Maddie!"

There was a scraping of key in lock then. She stuffed TD into her pocket and stood up, smoothing her apron, ready to resume for these last few hours her role as Maggie Hatley, airship parlourmaid.

EVIL EYE STRIKES! HORROR IN THE SKIES!

The cunning murderer of Baron Bodmin met a terrible fate off the shores of America yesterday. Our intrepid investigative reporter, W.Y. Knott, has been on his trail for weeks and witnessed his horrifying end.

While stealing a legendary diamond from a passenger's safe, disgraced Colonel Bilious Muster fell to his death from a White Sky Line airship en route to New York City. During the theft, the colonel violently assaulted a maid and a passenger who came to her aid.

A close friend to Baron Bodmin, Muster was the first person to learn of his success at tracking the Nubian mask known as the Eye of Africa. This mask's third eye is a large diamond, reputed to glow red when touched by evil, and some scholars claim the black face was streaked with the blood of murderers to enhance its power.

With his reputation and finances in chaos, Muster first absconded to Cornwall to greet his victorious friend. There, by devious means, he lured the exhausted explorer aboard his own airship and killed him. However, finding the mask was not aboard, he threw the baron and all evidence of his successful quest into the sea before escaping the vessel himself. The Jules Verne *was found adrift off Cornwall a few days later, and brought in by the Coast Guard.*

Muster then hid out at Bodmin Manor, searching for the mask. His unfruitful hunt was interrupted when the body came ashore and the baron's heir and investors arrived to claim their due. One of the latter found the mask and smuggled it out of England on a trans-oceanic White Sky Liner.

Muster may have overheard plans for the export of the mask, or simply hoped to evade the noose. However it came about, he talked his way into a position on the same ship, and departed England for America.

Waiting on opportunity, the erstwhile high-altitude scout set up a daring aerial escape route and, as the coast of the continent approached, assailed the safe that held the Eye of Africa.

Circumstance brought a maid into the room during his robbery. Although brutally flung about and half throttled, she was able to scream and a passerby rushed in to draw off her attacker. Muster turned his rage onto the newcomer and the maid, recovering her senses, rescued the unfortunate Good Samaritan.

In the struggle, Colonel Muster retrieved the mask and ran to his getaway craft. By then this reporter was on the scene and what follows is an exact accounting of the murderer's demise:

Colonel Muster carried the mask in one scratched and bleeding hand as he climbed onto his craft's wing. The diamond glowed red, faintly at first and then with a blinding heat. Muster flung up a hand to shield his face and lost his grip on the aircraft. He staggered and fell toward the sea, a thousand feet and more below.

The mask fell with him and is presumed lost to history. This reporter has no explanation for the red glow of the Eye, and must allow the images here shown to stand as surety for the truth of this account.